Honey and Homicide:
Alphabet Soup Mysteries

Book 8

Erica J Whelton

Publisher: Sunseri Design Publishing
Cover Designer: Mariah Sinclair Book Cover Design
ISBN: 978-1-956069-42-6

Printed in the United States of America

To the honeybees of the world

Chapter One

I fumbled with my keys at the front door, grocery bags cutting into my fingers while Ivy and Dove jostled on either side of me.

"I can help!" Ivy reached for a bag.

"Me too!" Dove grabbed for another.

"Hold on, hold on. Let me get the door open first before we drop everything on the porch."

The lock clicked and all three of us tumbled inside. I kicked the door shut with my heel and headed straight for the kitchen, the twins trailing behind like ducklings. The open floor plan meant I could see straight through from the kitchen to the front door, and anyone coming in had a clear view of the kitchen island.

"What's for dinner?" Ivy asked, already eyeing the grocery bags.

"Spaghetti and meatballs," I said, setting the bags on the counter.

"With garlic bread?" Ivy asked hopefully.

"And salad!" Dove added.

"Of course. Just how y'all like it." I smiled at them.

"Yay!" they chorused.

"But homework first, then snacks," I said.

Twin groans answered me.

"I know, I know. But that's the rule. Get started."

They pulled their homework folders from their backpacks while I started unpacking groceries. Ground beef for the meatballs, pasta, a fresh loaf for garlic bread, salad fixings. My phone buzzed. A text from Shayla: **Running a little late. Maybe 6:30?**

I replied with a thumbs up and glanced at the clock. 3:45. Plenty of time.

I noticed an earlier text from Kyle I'd missed that morning: **Good morning, beautiful. Thinking about you today. Hope work goes smoothly.**

I felt warmth spread through my chest. After our breakup during the Garrett Majors case, when the stress and accusations had driven a wedge between us, we'd worked hard to rebuild our relationship. It felt stronger now, more intentional. We communicated better, made time for each other despite our demanding schedules, and didn't let work cases come between us.

The breakup had been painful. For a month, Kyle had become so professional and distant when I was a suspect, treating me like a stranger when I'd needed him most. We'd both said things we regretted. But after the case was solved, we'd had long, honest conversations about what went wrong and what we both needed from the relationship.

Kyle had admitted he'd been terrified of showing favoritism, of compromising the investigation, but in trying to be completely professional, he'd shut me out entirely. I'd admitted I'd expected him to choose me over his job, which wasn't fair either.

Now, just a few weeks after getting back together, we'd found a better balance. He still took his job seriously, but he also made sure I knew he was there for me. And I understood the position he'd been in, even if it had hurt at the time.

I typed back: **Tomorrow night still good?**

His response came immediately: **Wouldn't miss it. Pizza and ice cream?**

I smiled. We had a standing Tuesday dinner tradition now, something we'd started as part of rebuilding our relationship. One night a week, no matter what, was ours. Sometimes it was just pizza on the couch with the twins, sometimes it was a real date. But it was consistent, and that consistency had helped us both feel secure again.

Perfect. The twins will be excited to see you, I typed.

Tell them I'm bringing their favorite cookies from Honey's Sweet Treats too, he replied, followed by a heart emoji.

My smile widened. Kyle remembered how much the twins loved those honey lavender cookies from Honey's bakery. It was the little things like this that reminded me why we'd worked so hard to rebuild what we'd almost lost.

"Math worksheets," Ivy announced, pulling out papers.

"Spelling words," Dove added.

I washed my hands and pulled out a container of cut vegetables with ranch dip. "Here, munch on these while you work."

"Carrots!" Dove grabbed one.

"And cucumbers!" Ivy took a handful.

I settled at the table between them, keeping one eye on homework and scrolling through my phone with the other. Ivy chewed her pencil, staring at a row of addition problems. Dove mouthed words silently, writing each one three times.

The front door opened at four o'clock sharp.

"Honey, I'm home!" Vee's voice rang out.

From the kitchen, I could see her standing in the doorway, her red curly hair pulled into a ponytail that had mostly escaped during the day. Frizzy tendrils framed her face. She was still in her postal uniform, looking tired but smiling.

"Hey, girls. How was school?" Vee walked toward the kitchen.

"Good!" they chorused.

"We're doing homework," Ivy said seriously.

"I see that. Very responsible." Vee grabbed a carrot from the container. "Jess, you're the best for having snacks ready."

"How was your day?" I asked.

"Busy. Everyone decided to mail packages today apparently." She plopped into a chair next to Dove. "But it's done now. Let me go change and I'll come help with homework."

"You don't have to do that."

"I want to!" Vee was already heading for the stairs. "Be right back!"

I smiled. Vee was barely five feet tall and looked like she could be blown over by a strong wind, but she had the biggest heart of anyone I knew. Patient, kind, and always ready to help.

Five minutes later, Vee returned in yoga pants and an oversized t-shirt, her hair freed from the ponytail and forming a wild halo around her head.

"Okay, who needs help?" She settled back at the table.

"I'm almost done," Ivy said, writing her last answer.

"Me too!" Dove finished her final spelling word with a flourish.

"Then how about you both read to me?" Vee suggested. "I love story time."

The twins scrambled to grab their reading books while I started browning the ground beef. I could hear Vee making exaggerated gasps and comments as first Dove, then Ivy, read their assigned pages.

"And then the dragon swooped down!" Dove read dramatically.

"No way!" Vee gasped. "What happened next?"

I smiled as I shaped meatballs and added them to a baking sheet. The familiar sounds of my makeshift family filled the kitchen with warmth. I slid the meatballs into the oven and started the water boiling for pasta.

At 6:35, the front door opened again. Through the open layout, I could see Shayla step inside. Her blonde hair was pulled back in a messy bun, and even from across the room, I could see the tension in her shoulders. Her eyes were red-rimmed.

"Shayla!" The twins jumped up.

Shayla's face transformed into a smile for her sisters, but it didn't reach her eyes. "Hey, you two. How was your day?"

"Good! We did homework and read to Vee!"

"That's great." Shayla's gaze met mine over their heads. "I'll tell you later," she mouthed.

I nodded slightly, my stomach tightening. Something was wrong.

"Go wash your hands, both of you," Shayla said, forcing brightness into her voice. "Dinner smells amazing."

The twins scrambled off to the bathroom while Shayla sagged against the counter.

"Not yet," I said quietly. "Let's get through dinner first."

Shayla nodded, blinking back tears.

Dinner was louder than usual. I kept the conversation moving, asking about the twins' day, about their upcoming math test, about the butterfly unit they were studying. Vee helped, telling a funny story about a customer at the post office who tried to mail a potted plant.

Shayla picked at her food, managing to eat about half while making the right sounds at the right times. The twins didn't seem to notice anything amiss, too busy debating whether monarch butterflies or swallowtails were prettier.

After dinner, the twins cleared their plates without being asked, then begged to watch a show before bed.

"Thirty minutes," Shayla said. "Then bath time."

They raced to the living room, arguing over which episode to watch. A moment later, the TV blared to life. They had the volume up way too loud, as usual.

Vee, Shayla, and I worked together to clean up the kitchen in silence. Once the dishwasher was loaded and running, we settled at the table with fresh cups of coffee. From where we sat, I could see the twins curled up on the couch, completely absorbed in their show.

"Okay," I said quietly. "What happened?"

Shayla's eyes filled with tears. "Honey's bees. All of them. They're dead."

"What?" Vee kept her voice low, but I could hear the shock. "All of them? How?"

"I don't know." Shayla wiped her eyes with the back of her hand. "She found them this morning. Just, thousands of dead bees everywhere. All three hives completely destroyed."

I felt my stomach drop. I bought honey, eggs, and goat cheese from Honey's farm regularly. I received a delivery weekly, but I hadn't been out to her farm in a while. I knew Honey was passionate about her bees, talked about them like they were her children. And Shayla had been so happy at the bakery, finally finding a place where she felt valued and secure.

"We should go see her tomorrow," I said. "Bring her something. Let her know we're here for her."

"She'd like that." Shayla managed a small smile. "Thank you. Both of you."

"That's what family does," Vee said.

Shayla glanced at the clock on the wall and pushed back from the table. "Bath time, girls!" she called toward the living room.

A chorus of groans answered her, but the TV clicked off and little feet padded toward the stairs.

"I've got it from here," Shayla said, standing. "You two have done enough today."

After Shayla disappeared upstairs with the twins, Vee turned to me. "You're going to look into this, aren't you?"

"I don't know what I can do."

"Jess." Vee gave me a knowing look. "I've known you long enough. You've got that look."

"What look?"

"The one that says you're already trying to solve it."

I sighed. "Someone deliberately hurt Honey's business. And it's affecting people I care about. So yeah, I want to help."

"Just be careful. Remember what happened last time."

"I'm always careful."

Vee snorted. "Sure you are."

We sat in comfortable silence for a moment, listening to the sounds of bath time chaos upstairs. Splashing, giggling, Shayla's patient voice reminding them to wash behind their ears.

"I'm going to head up," Vee said, standing and stretching. "Early shift tomorrow."

"Night, Vee."

"Night. And Jess? Don't stay up too late plotting."

The house grew quiet around me. I checked the locks, turned off the downstairs lights, and headed up to my room. I changed into my pajamas, brushed my teeth, and climbed into bed.

But sleep didn't come easily. My mind kept circling back to the same questions.

Who would do such a thing? And why?

What had killed all those bees? Who had access to Honey's farm? Who would benefit from destroying her livelihood?

I didn't have answers. Not yet. But tomorrow I'd visit Honey, bring her something comforting, and find out what she knew. Maybe then I'd have something to go on.

A soft thump on the bed announced Baxter's arrival. He padded up to my chest, his white paws kneading gently against my collarbone as he settled into his favorite position. Within seconds, his purr motor started: a deep, rumbling vibration that I could feel through my whole body.

"Hey, buddy," I whispered, stroking his soft black fur. "Big day tomorrow."

He pushed his head against my hand, purring louder, his green eyes half-closed in contentment.

Lulu appeared at the foot of the bed, giving Baxter an affectionate look before curling up near my feet. She was less demonstrative than Baxter; she'd always been more independent, less cuddly. But I knew Lulu's presence was her own form of comfort, even if she wouldn't admit to needing human affection. The gray and white cat had adored Baxter from the moment I brought him inside, and I suspected they'd been friends through the window long before that, back when Baxter lived as a stray on our street.

"You two are my favorite," I murmured.

Baxter's purring intensified, the steady rhythm beginning to calm my racing thoughts. This was his superpower: this ability to sense when I was stressed and provide exactly the kind of comfort I needed. When I'd found him shivering in the rain outside our townhouse, scared and alone, I'd had no idea how much he would come to mean to our little family.

I closed my eyes, focusing on the warmth of Baxter on my chest and the gentle weight of Lulu at my feet. Tomorrow I'd visit Honey. Tomorrow I'd start figuring out what really happened. Tomorrow I'd see if there was anything I could do to help.

But tonight, I had my cats, my family sleeping safely down the hall, and Kyle's good-night text still warm on my phone: **Sweet dreams.**

My breathing began to sync with Baxter's purring. In and out. Steady and rhythmic. Slowly, finally, sleep began to pull me under.

Tomorrow the real work would begin.

Chapter Two

I woke to the sound of something crashing in the kitchen.

I bolted upright, heart pounding, then heard the unmistakable sound of Lulu's soft meow followed by a triumphant chirp from Baxter.

"Not again," I muttered, throwing off the covers.

I found them in the kitchen. Baxter sat innocently by his food bowl, his black and white tail wrapped neatly around his paws. Lulu rubbed against him affectionately, grooming his ears with her rough tongue.

On the floor near the counter lay my favorite coffee mug, shattered into a dozen pieces.

"Really?" I sighed, carefully stepping around the ceramic shards. "That was my Crock Pot opening day mug!"

Baxter looked up at me with those innocent green eyes and meowed softly, as if he had no idea how it happened.

"Right. It just jumped off the counter by itself." I grabbed the broom and dustpan from the closet. I'd rescued Baxter from a rainstorm six months ago, and from the moment I'd brought him inside, Lulu had been smitten. I suspected they'd known each other before, probably through the front window. Baxter had lived on our street for years as a stray, and Lulu spent hours watching the world outside. They must have been friends through the glass long before Baxter came to live with us permanently.

Now they were inseparable. Where Lulu went, Baxter followed, and vice versa. It was adorable, except when their morning antics resulted in broken dishware.

Lulu rubbed against my leg, purring loudly, then went back to grooming Baxter. He closed his eyes and leaned into her attention, his own purr motor starting up.

"Yeah, yeah. I know you love him. Even when he's a troublemaker." I swept up the broken ceramic, making a mental note to keep the good mugs in the cabinet from now on. "But maybe we should work on your coordination, buddy."

As if in agreement, both cats began grooming each other, a tangle of gray, white, and black fur in the morning sunlight streaming through the kitchen window.

"You two are ridiculous," I said, but I was smiling.

I settled for a plain blue mug for my coffee. It would have to do.

I was halfway through my coffee when I heard Shayla getting the twins ready for school. Muffled conversations about missing socks and forgotten homework drifted through the thin walls.

"Ivy, where's your backpack?"

"I don't know!"

"It's by the front door where it always is."

I smiled and checked my phone. 7:15. I had time before heading to The Crock Pot.

A text from Kyle was waiting: **Good morning, beautiful. Looking forward to tonight. What time should I come over?**

I typed back: **Morning! Around 6? That gives me time to pick up the twins and get home.**

His response came immediately: **Perfect. See you then. Love you.**

Love you too, I replied, my chest warming.

Lulu appeared at my feet, meowing for breakfast. I scratched the gray and white cat behind the ears. "Alright, alright. Let me get dressed first."

By the time I made it back downstairs after showering and getting dressed, Shayla was already loading the twins into her car parked at the curb. I waved through the kitchen window as they pulled away, then filled the cat bowls. Baxter and Lulu wound around my ankles, meowing impatiently, then settled in for breakfast side by side.

I made fresh coffee and toast, then sat at the kitchen island with my phone. I scrolled to Honey's contact and hesitated. It felt intrusive to bother someone who was grieving, but Shayla needed her job, and Honey needed support.

I typed: **Hi Honey, it's Jess. Shayla told me what happened. I'm so sorry. Would it be okay if I stopped by today? I'd like to bring you something.**

The response came back quickly: **Oh Jess, yes please. Could you come to the farm? I can't bear to be at the bakery today. Maybe around 4? I know you pick up the twins, but after that?**

Of course. See you then.

I arrived at The Crock Pot just before eight, pulling into my usual spot in the back lot. Noah's car was already there, which made me smile. We'd both been opening together for so long now that we had an unspoken competition about who could arrive first.

I found him in the kitchen, tablet already in hand, pulling up our inventory spreadsheet.

"Morning," I said, setting down my bag and tying on my apron.

"Morning." He took one look at me and raised an eyebrow. "You've got that look."

"What look?"

"The one where you're trying to solve something that isn't technically your problem." He pulled up his tablet. "Let me guess. Honey's bees?"

"Cullen told you?"

"He posted about it yesterday. Word travels fast in this town." Noah scrolled through his notes. "Poor woman. Years of work destroyed overnight."

"It's terrible."

"Hence the look." Noah's expression was dry. "You're already investigating, aren't you?"

"I'm going to visit her this afternoon. Bringing food."

"Of course you are." He made a note on his tablet, then gestured toward the walk-in cooler. "Well, while you're playing detective, I'll keep this place running. Want to knock out inventory together? That way you can prep while your mind wanders to murder."

"It's not murder. It's... agricultural sabotage?"

"Sure. We'll go with that." He was already walking toward the cooler. "Come on. Let's see what we're low on."

We spent the next hour working through inventory together, Noah calling out items while I counted and restocked. It was our usual morning rhythm, comfortable and efficient.

"We're good on proteins through Thursday," Noah said, making notes. "But we'll need more potatoes by Wednesday."

"I'll call the supplier."

"Already did. They're delivering tomorrow morning." He glanced up from his tablet. "Parker takes over at three, so you're covered if you need to leave early. And that new guy, Andy, is working with you on soups today. First day on his own station."

"How's he been doing in training?"

"Solid. Follows directions, good knife skills, doesn't panic when things get busy. I think he'll work out."

"Good. We needed the extra help."

"Eli's got grill covered, and I've already checked the prep list. We're good through the week."

"You're the best."

"I know. It's a burden I bear gracefully." His deadpan delivery made me smile despite everything.

By the time inventory was done, my mind had wandered back to Honey at least a dozen times. Who would do such a thing? And why?

Noah must have noticed because he said, "Go prep before the lunch rush hits and you don't have time to think about murder. Or agricultural sabotage. Whatever we're calling it."

"Thanks, Noah."

"See you at two." He was already walking away, tablet in hand, ready to tackle whatever the day threw at us.

The lunch rush kept me busy enough that I couldn't dwell too much on the case. Eli had the grill station running smoothly, and Andy managed the soup station better than I expected for someone still learning the ropes. I kept an eye on him between my own tasks, but he handled the pressure well.

At 3:00, I drove to Dashwood Elementary. The pickup line was already forming, a familiar ritual I'd come to enjoy.

The bell rang at three fifteen, and children poured out of the building. I spotted the twins immediately; Ivy's bright pink backpack and Dove's purple one making them easy to identify.

"Jess! Jess!" Ivy called through the window, waving enthusiastically.

"We learned about butterfly migration!" Dove added, climbing into the backseat.

"That sounds amazing. Tell me all about it."

The drive home was filled with their usual animated chatter. Monarchs flying thousands of miles. Multiple generations making the journey. How they navigated using the sun and an internal compass no one fully understood.

"It's like magic," Dove said, her eyes wide. "But it's real!"

"Science can be like that," I agreed. "The best kind of magic."

By the time I parked at the curb in front of our house, I was smiling despite the weight of everything else on my mind.

"Homework first," I said as we climbed the front steps.

"Can we have a snack?" Ivy asked.

"Of course. But homework while you eat."

I got them settled at the kitchen table with apple slices and peanut butter, supervised the start of their math worksheets, then went upstairs to prepare the basket I'd planned for Honey. I'd made the rolls early this morning before leaving for work. The soup, a hearty vegetable beef, and the casserole, chicken and rice that could be frozen for later, I'd brought home from The Crock Pot, already packed in containers.

Comfort food. The kind that said "I care" without requiring words.

At 3:45, Vee came through the front door, her curly red hair even more disheveled than usual, escaping in wild tendrils from her ponytail.

"Rough day?" I asked.

"Package got lost, customer yelled at me for twenty minutes like it was my fault." Vee plopped down next to Dove. "But I'm here now. How was everyone's day?"

"Good! We learned about butterflies!" the twins chorused.

"Want to hear about them while I'm gone?" I asked. "I'm going to visit Honey at her farm."

"Of course. We've got this covered." Vee was already looking at Ivy's math problems. "Ooh, multiplication. I can help with that."

I grabbed the basket and my purse. "There are more vegetables and hummus in the fridge if they want extra snacks. Shayla should be home by six."

"Go. We're fine here." Vee shooed me toward the door. "Give Honey our love."

I drove out to Honey J's Farm and Flowers, the basket of food on the passenger seat filling my car with the warm scent of fresh bread. The farm sat on about ten acres just outside Dashwood's city limits, accessible by a winding two-lane road that cut through gently rolling hills.

I'd been there once before, about six months ago, to pick up eggs and honey. I remembered thinking it looked like something from a country living magazine: neat rows of flowers in every color, a white farmhouse with a wraparound porch, a red barn. But what I remembered most vividly was the constant, busy hum of thousands of bees moving between the hives and flowers, the gentle buzz of industrious life filling the air. It had been mesmerizing to watch them work, small dark shapes dancing from blossom to blossom.

Today, the charm felt muted. Even from the gravel road, approaching the property, something felt off. The flowers were still there, bright and blooming, but the air was silent. No buzzing. No movement of bees among the petals. Just stillness where there should have been life.

I parked near the farmhouse and grabbed the basket. The front door opened before I could knock.

"Jess." Honey Jacobson stood in the doorway, and the transformation shocked me. Honey was usually robust and energetic, her graying brown hair pulled back in a practical ponytail, her face sun-kissed from outdoor work. Today, her hair hung loose and lank, her eyes were red and swollen, and she looked like she'd aged ten years.

"I'm so sorry, Honey." I handed over the basket. "I brought some things for you."

"You didn't have to do that." Honey's voice cracked as she looked into the basket. "But thank you. Come in, please."

The farmhouse kitchen was warm and inviting, with yellow walls, herbs growing on the windowsill, and a large wooden table that looked like a family heirloom. But even this cheerful space couldn't dispel the weight of grief that hung in the air.

"May's out back," Honey said, setting the basket on the counter with shaking hands. "She's trying to salvage what honey she can from the hives before it's ruined. We have to leave everything else alone until the expert comes, but the honey..." She trailed off, her voice breaking. "I can't look at it yet. I just can't."

Through the back window, I could see a woman in her thirties with short dark hair kneeling near what looked like wooden boxes.

Beehives. Even from this distance, dark shapes covered the ground around them.

"How long have you two been partners?" I asked gently.

"Three years now. She answered an ad I put up for help with the farm." Honey moved to the coffee pot, her movements slow and mechanical. "Turned out she had a background in agriculture and a real passion for sustainable farming. She knew about beekeeping, crop rotation, and organic pest management. All the things I wanted to do but didn't have the knowledge for."

Honey poured two cups of coffee, her hands shaking so badly that some slopped over the sides.

"I don't know what I would have done without her, especially this past year." Honey wiped her eyes with the back of her hand. "She's been my rock."

"Shayla mentioned you discovered them yesterday morning?"

"May found them first. She's always up and out in the fields before I've even had my coffee, likes to check on things before the heat sets in." Honey handed me a mug and clutched her own like a lifeline. "She called me from the hives, screaming. Actual screaming. I thought someone had been hurt, thought maybe she'd fallen and broken something."

Honey stared out the window at May, who was still kneeling by the hives.

"When I got here, she was just standing there among all those dead bees, crying. I've never seen her cry before. May's tough, you know? Farm tough. But she was just... destroyed."

I accepted the coffee, wrapping my hands around the warm mug. "Do you have any idea what could have caused it?"

"The county extension office is sending someone in a few days. An expert in bee diseases and pests. Maybe he'll have answers." Honey's voice was flat, devoid of hope. "May thinks it was deliberate. She keeps saying bees don't just all die like that, not overnight, not without warning."

"Do the police know?"

"They came by yesterday. Took some photos, asked questions. But they said until the expert determines what happened, there's not much they can do." Honey's hands trembled around her mug. "They're calling it 'suspicious circumstances,' whatever that means."

"I'm so sorry."

We sat in silence for a moment, the only sound the ticking of an old clock on the wall and the distant sound of May moving around outside.

"This farm is my life," Honey said finally. "The bees, the flowers, the bakery. It's all connected. Without the bees, the flowers won't produce like they should. Without the honey and the flowers, the bakery loses what makes it special. And without any of it..." She trailed off, unable or unwilling to finish the thought.

I reached across the table and squeezed Honey's hand. "We'll figure this out. You're not alone in this."

"I keep telling myself that. But late at night, when I can't sleep, it feels like I am." Honey's eyes filled with fresh tears. "This land has been in my family for three generations, Jess. My grandmother built this farm. My mother expanded it. When I inherited it, I saw even more possibilities. The bees, the flowers, the bakery using our own honey. I brought May in as a partner because she had the agricultural expertise I needed to make that vision real. And now someone might have taken it all away."

"Has anyone been bothering you?" I asked. "Asking questions about your operation?"

Honey hesitated, then set her mug down. "There was a man who came into the bakery a few weeks ago. He made me uncomfortable, the way he was asking such specific questions about the farm, about how much land I had, whether I was thinking of selling. But I never thought... I never imagined someone would actually do something like this."

"What did he look like?"

"Shayla was the one who waited on him at first. I came out from the back when I heard all the questions he was asking." Honey rubbed her temples. "Middle-aged, maybe fifties or sixties? Tall, weathered looking. He had on a baseball cap, so I didn't get a great look at his face. But there was something about him, the way he talked, like he was used to being in charge. I tried to give short answers, change the subject, but he kept pushing."

"Did he give a name?"

"No. Paid cash and left. But Shayla said she saw him sitting in his truck outside for a while afterward, just watching the building."

"Do you remember when this was?"

"About two weeks ago? Maybe three? Time's been a blur lately."

I pulled out my phone and made a note. "Has anyone else shown unusual interest? Asked about your schedule, when you check the hives, anything like that?"

Honey thought for a moment. "Not that I can think of. Most people who come by are regular customers or people interested in learning about beekeeping. I give tours sometimes, talk about the process. But no one's been pushy or weird about it."

"What about competitors? Other beekeepers or flower growers in the area?"

"There's a couple in Pinehurst who do flowers, but we've always been friendly. And the nearest beekeeper is over in Moore County. We help each other out when we can, share tips and equipment." Honey's voice broke. "This isn't about competition. This is personal. Someone wanted to hurt me specifically."

The back door opened and May stepped inside, her boots muddy and her face streaked with dirt and tears. She froze when she saw me.

"Oh. I didn't know we had company."

"May, this is Jess Vasquez. Shayla's... guardian, I guess? She owns The Crock Pot."

"Nice to meet you," May said quietly, moving to the sink to wash her hands. "Sorry, I'm a mess."

"Don't apologize," I said. "I can't imagine how difficult this is."

May dried her hands and leaned against the counter, looking exhausted. "I've been working with bees for fifteen years. I've seen diseases, parasites, colony collapse. But I've never seen anything like this. The way they died, all at once, all three hives..." She shook her head. "This wasn't natural."

"Do you think someone poisoned them?" I asked.

"That's my best guess. Some kind of pesticide, maybe, or a toxin introduced directly into the hives." May's eyes narrowed. "Whoever did this knew what they were doing. They knew when to strike, how to get close without being seen. This wasn't some random act of vandalism."

I felt a chill run down my spine. "You really think someone planned this?"

"I know they did. Bees don't just die like this overnight. Not all three hives at once. Someone targeted us specifically."

Honey started crying again, and May immediately moved to comfort her, wrapping an arm around her shoulders.

"We'll rebuild," May said firmly. "We'll get new bees, start over. We won't let whoever did this win."

But I saw the fear in both their eyes. Fear that starting over might not be possible. Fear that whoever had done this might strike again.

The sound of tires on gravel made all three of us look toward the window. A large pickup truck, a Ford F-250 with a lift kit, was pulling up the drive. The man behind the wheel wore a John Deere cap and had the weathered look of someone who worked outdoors.

Honey's expression shifted from grief to something harder. "Clark."

"Who's Clark?" I asked.

"Clark Marlowe. He owns the property next to ours." Honey's voice was tight. "He's been trying to buy my land for over a year now."

The truck door slammed, and I watched Clark Marlowe stride toward the house. He was probably in his fifties, with a ruddy face and broad shoulders. His boots were muddy, and he brought with him the smell of diesel fuel and earth.

Honey opened the kitchen door before he could knock. "Clark. Now isn't a good time."

"I heard what happened." Clark pulled off his cap and held it against his chest in a gesture that was probably meant to look sympathetic. "Terrible thing. Just terrible. I wanted to come by and offer my condolences."

"Thank you." Honey's tone was flat.

Clark's eyes swept past her to take in May and me. He nodded at May, then his gaze lingered on me with curiosity. "Don't think we've met. Clark Marlowe."

"Jessica Vasquez." I didn't offer my hand.

"The chef? The one who owns The Crock Pot?" His eyebrows rose. "Heard a lot about you. The crime-fighting chef, they call you."

"I'm just here to support a friend."

"Of course, of course." Clark turned back to Honey, his expression shifting to something that looked almost eager beneath the mask of sympathy. "Listen, Honey, I know this isn't the time, but I want you to know my offer still stands. In fact, given the circumstances, I'd be willing to go higher. Four hundred thousand, cash. You could walk away clean, start over somewhere else."

My stomach turned. The man's livelihood-destroying "tragedy" had barely cooled, and he was already circling like a vulture.

Honey's face went pale, then flushed with anger. "Clark, my bees died yesterday. Yesterday. And you're here talking about buying my land?"

"I'm just saying, you've got options. No need to struggle when you don't have to." Clark spread his hands in a gesture of false reasonableness. "Think about it. That's all I'm asking."

"I think you should leave," May said, stepping forward. Her voice was cold.

Clark looked between the three of us, then shrugged and put his cap back on. "Just trying to help. You know where to find me when you're ready to talk sense."

He turned and walked back to his truck, whistling softly under his breath. The casual cruelty of it made my blood boil.

As his truck pulled away, Honey sank into a chair, her hands shaking. "He's been after this land since the day I bought it. Says small operations like mine aren't sustainable, that I'd be better off selling to him."

"That's awfully convenient timing," I said quietly. "Him showing up the day after your bees are destroyed."

Honey looked up at me, her eyes widening as the implication sank in. "You don't think... Clark can be pushy, but would he really do something like this?"

"I don't know," I said honestly. "But it's worth mentioning to the police."

May was still staring out the window at the dust settling from Clark's truck. "I wouldn't put anything past that man. He's been pressuring Honey for months. Every time she says no, he comes back with a higher offer. It's harassment."

"Has he ever threatened you?" I asked.

"Not directly," Honey said. "But he's made comments. About how hard it is to run a small farm alone. How accidents happen. How the market can be unpredictable." She wrapped her arms around herself. "I always thought he was just being a pest. But now..."

I made a mental note to look into Clark Marlowe more closely. The timing of his visit, the way he'd talked about Honey's "tragedy" like it was an opportunity. Something about the man felt deeply wrong.

After finishing my coffee and promising to check in tomorrow, I drove home with my mind racing. Someone had deliberately destroyed Honey's livelihood. Someone with knowledge, resources, and a reason to want Honey's business to fail.

Clark Marlowe's face kept appearing in my mind. The way he'd shown up so quickly after the tragedy. The eager glint in his eyes when he'd made his offer. The casual cruelty of his timing.

Was he capable of destroying those hives? He certainly had motive; he wanted Honey's land. And he seemed like the type who wouldn't let ethics stand in the way of getting what he wanted.

But I was getting ahead of myself. I didn't even know yet what had killed the bees. Until the expert came, everything was speculation.

Still, I couldn't shake the feeling that Clark Marlowe was hiding something. And I intended to find out what.

Chapter Three

By the time I pulled into my parking spot at the curb, I had more questions than answers. But I was determined to find the truth, no matter what it took.

I sat in the car for a moment, staring at the townhouse. Through the front window, I could see movement inside. The twins doing homework, probably. Vee home from work. Normal, everyday life continuing despite the horror I'd just witnessed at Honey's farm.

My phone buzzed. A text from Kyle: **How did it go? Are you okay?**

I typed back: **Just got home. It was rough. Really rough.**

Kyle: I'm sorry. Still on for tonight? I can reschedule if you need time.

Me: No, please come. I need the normalcy. Need you.

Kyle: Be there in twenty minutes. Love you.

Love you too, I replied, my chest warming. This Kyle, the one who checked in and made sure I was okay while still respecting our plans, was so different from the distant, professional version I'd dealt with during the Garrett Majors case. We'd learned so much since then.

Inside, the house was controlled chaos. Ivy and Dove were at the kitchen table, math worksheets spread out in front of them. Vee was helping Dove with multiplication while simultaneously trying to keep Baxter from walking across the papers.

"Baxter, no!" Vee gently moved the black and white cat aside. He promptly sat down and began grooming himself, offended.

"How's Honey?" Shayla asked from the couch, where she'd clearly been anxiously waiting.

"Devastated. I'll tell you more later." I glanced at the twins, who were absorbed in their homework. "Kyle's coming over in a bit."

"On a Tuesday?" Vee raised an eyebrow, then grinned. "Oh wait, it IS Tuesday. Pizza night!"

"Exactly."

Twenty minutes later, right on time, Kyle knocked on the door. I could see him through the window, still in his uniform, holding two grocery bags.

"Kyle!" Dove abandoned her homework the moment I opened the door, launching herself at him.

"Hey there, Miss Dove." Kyle caught her with one arm, somehow managing not to drop the bags. "How was school?"

"Good! We're learning multiplication!"

"That's great. Is your sister around?"

"I'm here!" Ivy appeared, pushing past me. "Did you bring cookies from Miss Honey's?"

Kyle's expression flickered, just for a second, and I knew he was thinking about the destroyed hives, about how there might not be a Honey's Sweet Treats much longer. But he recovered quickly, holding up the bags.

"I sure did. And pizza. And ice cream. Figured we all deserved a treat tonight."

"Ice cream!" both twins cheered.

Kyle's eyes met mine over their heads, and his smile widened.

I stepped aside, letting him in. "Perfect timing."

"Yay!" The twins ran back to clear their homework off the table.

"Hey, Kyle," Shayla called from the couch, managing a small smile.

"Hey, Shayla. How are you holding up?"

"Been better. But I'm glad you're here."

Kyle set the bags on the kitchen counter. "Pizza should still be hot. Polly's was packed, so I'm lucky I got it when I did."

"You're the best," I said, pulling out plates.

Baxter appeared from his spot by the window, immediately weaving between Kyle's legs and purring loudly. Lulu watched from her perch on the windowsill, too dignified to beg for attention but clearly interested in the evening's developments.

"Hey, buddy." Kyle crouched down to scratch Baxter behind the ears. "Did you miss me?"

"He always sits by the door on Tuesdays," Ivy said matter-of-factly. "Waiting for you."

Kyle glanced up at me, something soft and vulnerable in his expression. "That right?"

"News to me, but apparently yes," I said, watching Baxter lean into Kyle's hand, purring like a motor.

"Well, I'm glad to see you too, pal."

We crowded around the kitchen table, passing plates and napkins, the twins chattering about their day. It felt surreal, this normalcy, after what I'd seen at the farm. But it also felt necessary. A reminder that life continued, that there was still goodness and laughter and family dinners, even when the world felt dark.

Kyle had ordered two large pepperoni and mushroom pizzas, the twins' favorite, and a small Hawaiian for Vee, who had weird pizza preferences. The smell of melted cheese and warm bread filled the kitchen, making my stomach growl. I hadn't realized how hungry I was until that moment.

"So," Kyle said, helping Dove get a slice onto her plate without dropping it, "tell me about these butterflies you learned about today."

And just like that, the twins were off, talking over each other about monarch migration, how they traveled thousands of miles, how multiple generations made the journey.

"They use the sun like a compass," Ivy explained seriously. "And they have a magnetic thing in their brains."

"Magnetoreception," Dove corrected. "That's what Ms. Henderson called it."

"That's amazing," Kyle said, and he meant it. I could see the genuine interest in his eyes as he listened to them.

After we finished eating, Kyle unpacked the ice cream: chocolate chip cookie dough, mint chocolate chip, strawberry, and butter pecan.

"You got all our favorites," Shayla said softly, her eyes glistening. The stress of the day was written all over her face, but she managed a smile.

"I pay attention," Kyle said simply, scooping strawberry into a bowl for her.

We ate ice cream and talked about nothing important. Vee shared the saga of a customer at the post office who'd tried to mail a live plant. The twins debated whether butterflies or moths were cooler. Shayla laughed at something Dove said, some of the tension leaving her shoulders.

I watched Kyle across the table, the way he listened to everyone like what they were saying was the most important thing in the world. The way he made sure everyone got their favorite flavor before taking any for himself. The way he caught my eye and smiled, small and private, like we were sharing a secret.

This. This was what I'd been terrified of losing during the Garrett Majors case. Not just Kyle, but this, the easiness of him being here, being part of our strange little family unit. The way he fit, like he'd always belonged here.

"Jess?" Kyle's voice pulled me back to the present. "You okay?"

"Yeah. Just thinking."

"Thinking looks serious on you."

"Sometimes thinking is serious."

"Fair point." He scraped the last of his butter pecan from the bowl, then glanced at his watch. "I should probably get going. Early shift tomorrow."

"Aw, do you have to?" Dove asked.

"Unfortunately, yes. But I'll see you soon, okay?"

The twins hugged him goodbye, sticky fingers and all. Vee gave him a knowing look that made him duck his head. Shayla thanked him quietly for the pizza and ice cream, for being there, for caring about all of them.

"Walk me out?" Kyle asked me.

I followed him outside, closing the door behind us. The evening air was cool, carrying the scent of honeysuckle from a neighbor's yard. The sun was setting, painting the sky in shades of orange and pink.

We stood on the small landing at the top of the steps, close together in the limited space.

"Thank you for tonight," I said. "I needed this more than I realized."

"Me too." Kyle's hand found mine, his thumb tracing circles on my palm. "How are you? Really?"

"Tired. Sad for Honey. Worried about Shayla." I sighed. "And trying not to spiral into full investigation mode before I even know what I'm investigating."

"That's very restrained of you."

"I'm learning."

"We both are." Kyle stepped closer, his free hand coming up to cup my cheek. "What you saw today at the farm, it was bad. It made my stomach drop."

"Worse than I expected. Kyle, whoever did this, they didn't just destroy the hives. They destroyed something Honey loved. It was cruel."

His jaw tightened. "I'm meeting with Dr. Fry tomorrow morning. The bee expert from the county extension office. We need to know exactly what killed those bees before we can figure out who did it."

"May thinks it was deliberate. She said bees don't just die like that overnight, not all three hives at once."

"That's what we're hoping Dr. Fry can confirm."

My phone buzzed. I glanced at the screen. "It's Honey."

Honey: The police told me the bee expert is coming tomorrow at 10. I don't think I can face this news alone. Would you be able to come?

I showed Kyle the message. "She wants me there tomorrow. I'll stay out of your way, just be there to support her."

"That's fine. She could use a friendly face." He squeezed my hand. "And Jess, I need you to promise me something."

"What?"

"If you start investigating, and I know you will, because that's who you are, be careful. Whoever did this had knowledge, resources, and a specific plan. They're not some random vandal. They're dangerous."

"I'll be careful."

"I'm serious." His thumb brushed across my cheekbone. "I can't go through another case like Garrett Majors. Watching you put yourself in danger, not being able to be there for you because of protocol and evidence and all the rules I thought mattered more than us." His voice roughened. "I was wrong. You matter more. This matters more."

My throat tightened with emotion. "Kyle..."

"I know we said we'd take things one day at a time, that we wouldn't make big declarations. But I need you to know that I'm all in. Whatever happens with this case, with any case, I'm not going anywhere. Not again."

"I'm all in too," I whispered.

He kissed me then, soft and sweet and tasting like butter pecan. When he pulled back, his forehead rested against mine.

"Promise me you'll be careful," he said again.

"I promise. And you promise too. No shutting me out if things get complicated."

"I promise. We communicate this time. About everything." He kissed my forehead. "Even when it's hard."

"Especially when it's hard."

He smiled, that soft smile that was just for me. "I should go before I don't want to leave."

"Would that be so bad?"

"Yes, because I have to be up at five, and I know if I stay we'll end up talking until midnight."

"Fair point."

He kissed me one more time, quick and light, then jogged down the steps to his cruiser. I watched until his taillights disappeared around the corner, my fingers touching my lips.

When I came back inside, Vee was loading the dishwasher, a knowing smile on her face. "That man is gone for you."

"I know."

"And you're gone for him."

"I know that too."

"Good." Vee closed the dishwasher and turned to face me. "After everything you two went through, you deserve this. You both do."

"Thanks, Vee."

"Now, you want to tell me what you really saw at the farm today? Once the twins are in bed?"

I glanced toward the living room, where Shayla was getting the twins ready for their bath. "Yeah. And we're going to need the murder board."

"I figured. I'll make coffee."

Chapter Four

Vee started a fresh pot of coffee while I checked on the twins. Shayla had them halfway through their bath, Ivy making a bubble beard while Dove splashed her sister playfully.

"Jess! Look!" Ivy pointed to her foamy chin. "I'm Santa!"

"Very distinguished," I said. "Finish up, okay? Story time soon."

I returned to the kitchen where Vee was pouring two mugs. "They're almost done. Shayla's got it handled."

"Good. Because we have work to do." Vee handed me a mug and nodded toward the stairs. "Murder board?"

"Let me wait for Shayla. I want to ask her some questions about the bakery first."

By eight o'clock, Ivy and Dove were in their pajamas, teeth brushed, and tucked into their beds in the downstairs bedroom.

"Story time!" Dove called from their room.

"Coming!" Shayla called back, grabbing their favorite book from the coffee table.

Thirty minutes later, Shayla emerged from the twins' room, looking exhausted. She dropped onto the couch next to Vee and me, where we were both scrolling through our phones.

"They asleep?" Vee asked.

"Finally. Ivy kept asking about when Riley and Sawyer's baby shower would be. I think they're more excited about that than anything else right now."

"That's good. Normal kid stuff." I set my phone aside. "How are you holding up? With everything at the bakery, I mean."

Shayla's face crumpled slightly. "I'm scared, Jess. Really scared. This job means everything to us. The hours are perfect, Honey treats me well, and I actually love what I do there. If the bakery closes..."

"Hey." I reached over and squeezed Shayla's hand. "You know you always have a place at The Crock Pot, right? I know the hours wouldn't be ideal with the twins, but we'd figure something out."

"I know you'd try, but your evening shift doesn't work for us. And I can't ask you to completely restructure your business for me."

"You're not asking. I'm offering. We're family, Shayla. We figure things out together."

Shayla's eyes filled with tears. "Thank you. That means more than you know."

We sat in comfortable silence for a moment, the weight of unspoken worries hanging between us.

"Can I ask you something?" I said. "Have you noticed anyone unusual around the bakery lately? Anyone asking questions about Honey or the farm?"

Shayla frowned, thinking. "Actually, yes. There was someone a few weeks ago. A man came in asking a lot of questions about Honey's operation. At first, I thought he was just a curious customer, you know? People love hearing about the farm and the bees."

"But?"

"But his questions were different. More specific. He wanted to know how many hives she had, what kind of security she used, and how often she checked on them. It felt... probing. Like he was gathering information rather than just being curious."

I felt my pulse quicken. "What did he look like?"

"Middle-aged, maybe fifties or sixties? Tall, kind of weathered looking. He had on a baseball cap, so I didn't get a great look at his face. But he had this way of talking, like he was used to being in charge."

"That sounds suspicious," Vee said, leaning forward. "Did Honey talk to him?"

"A little. She came out from the back when she heard him asking about the farm. She was polite, but I could tell she wasn't comfortable with all his questions. She kept giving short answers and trying to change the subject."

"Did he buy anything?"

"A coffee and a muffin. But he spent more time asking questions than eating. And when he left, I saw him sitting in his truck outside for a while, just looking at the building."

My mind was racing. Who was this man, and what did he want with Honey's farm?

"Did you get a look at his truck?"

"Big pickup. Dark colored, maybe blue or black? I'm not great with car stuff." Shayla paused. "Why? Do you think he had something to do with what happened to the bees?"

"I don't know. Maybe. It's just suspicious timing, you know? Someone asking detailed questions about Honey's security, and then a few weeks later, all her bees are dead."

"That's terrifying," Shayla said. "To think someone was planning this for weeks."

"At least Honey already called the police," Vee added. "She told you they came out yesterday, right? So they're taking it seriously."

"They are, but they said there's not much they can do until the expert determines what actually killed the bees." I thought about what Kyle had said on the porch. "Kyle mentioned he's meeting with the bee expert tomorrow morning. Dr. Fry from the county extension office."

"Will they figure out who did it?" Shayla asked.

"That's the goal. Once we know how the bees died, it might point us toward who's responsible."

"Do you really think someone planned this?" Shayla asked quietly.

I thought about the man who'd asked probing questions about security and then sat in his truck watching the bakery. About Honey's fear that this was personal.

"I think," I said carefully, "that someone wanted Honey to fail. And killing her bees was a pretty effective way to make that happen."

The three of us sat in sobering silence, each lost in our own thoughts about what kind of person would destroy someone's livelihood for their own gain.

Outside, the wind picked up, rattling the windows.

After the conversation wound down, Shayla headed to bed, exhausted from the emotional day. I sat on the couch for a few more minutes, my mind spinning with everything we'd discussed.

"You're thinking really loud over there," Vee said, closing her book. "Want to talk about it?"

"Yes, but now that I've talked to Shayla, let's go start that murder board."

Vee's eyes lit up. "Absolutely."

We climbed the stairs quietly, careful not to wake the twins or Shayla. In my room, I pulled out the poster board from its hiding place in the closet and laid it on the bed. Lulu and Baxter, who'd been sleeping on the comforter, immediately relocated to investigate.

"Shoo, you two," I said, gently moving them aside. "This is important work."

Baxter settled on my pillow, watching with interest. Lulu curled up at the foot of the bed, pretending not to care but keeping one eye open.

Vee studied the blank board. "Okay, let's start with what we know. The basics first."

I grabbed a marker and a fresh set of sticky notes. At the top, I wrote: Honey J's Farm, Bees Killed. Below that: Three hives destroyed. Found Monday morning by May. Police called Monday. Expert coming Wednesday.

"Now the suspicious customer," I said, starting a new note. "Shayla's description goes here." I wrote it out: Middle-aged man, 50s-60s, tall, weathered, baseball cap. Asked specific questions about security, hives, schedule. Dark pickup truck. Watched bakery after leaving.

"That's creepy," Vee said. "And definitely premeditated."

"Right. This wasn't someone acting on impulse. They were gathering intel." I stuck the note under the Suspicious Activity section.

"What about suspects?" Vee asked. "Who benefits from Honey's farm failing?"

I thought for a moment, then started a new section: Suspects.

"Well, there's whoever that customer was. We don't know his name yet, but maybe Honey or the police can help identify him."

I wrote: Unknown man from bakery. Middle-aged, tall, weathered. Drove dark pickup. Motive unknown.

"Who else?" Vee prompted.

"I don't know yet. We need more information about who else might have a motive." I tapped the marker against my chin. "Competing businesses? Someone with a grudge? Has anyone been trying to buy Honey's property?"

"Good question. You should ask her tomorrow."

I added it to the board: Who else has motive? Competitors? Grudges? Property buyers?

"What about May?" Vee asked quietly.

I looked at my friend, surprised. "Honey's farm partner?"

"Think about it. Shayla said Honey seemed uncomfortable when the man was asking questions. But did May seem uncomfortable? And they're partners, right? So, if the farm fails, what happens?"

I felt a chill. "I don't know. I'd have to find out what their partnership agreement says."

"Just something to consider," Vee said. "I'm not saying she did it, but in mysteries, you always look at who stands to gain."

I added a tentative note: May Lowen, Farm partner. Financial situation? Partnership terms?

"What about timeline?" Vee pointed to the Questions section. "We know the man came to the bakery a few weeks ago. When did Honey last check the hives before finding them dead?"

"Good question." I added it to the board: When were hives last checked before attack? When did bees die?

"And we need to know what actually killed them," Vee added. "The expert comes tomorrow. That should give us answers."

I made another note: Expert findings, what killed the bees? How?

We worked in comfortable silence for a few more minutes, adding questions and organizing information. Baxter eventually got bored and padded over to rub against my hand, demanding attention.

"Okay, buddy. I get it. Bedtime." I scratched behind his ears, and he started purring.

Vee stepped back to look at the completed board. "This is good. We're actually starting to build a picture."

"A scary picture," I said. "Someone spent weeks planning this attack. That level of calculation is terrifying."

"Which is why we need to figure out who did it before they do something worse." Vee helped me carefully fold the board and tuck it back into the closet. "Get some sleep. Tomorrow we meet the expert and hopefully get some real answers."

After Vee left, I changed into my pajamas and climbed into bed. Baxter immediately claimed his spot on my chest, purring steadily. Lulu settled near my feet, a warm, comforting weight.

I closed my eyes, but my mind kept returning to the board. To the suspects, the questions, the timeline of someone's calculated attack on Honey's livelihood.

Tomorrow we'd know more. Tomorrow the expert would tell us what killed those bees. And tomorrow, I'd start getting real answers.

But tonight, I had my cats, my family safe under the same roof, and Kyle's promise still warm in my mind: We communicate this time. About everything.

I fell asleep to the sound of Baxter's purring, determined that tomorrow would bring us closer to the truth.

Chapter Five

The next morning, I dropped the twins at school after Shayla left for work. Honey had decided to keep the bakery open, wanting to maintain some sense of normalcy while she dealt with the crisis at the farm.

At 9:50, I pulled into the gravel drive at Honey J's Farm and Flowers, wanting to arrive a few minutes before the expert was scheduled. Two police cars were already there, along with Kyle's cruiser near the farmhouse. No other unfamiliar vehicles yet. The expert must not have arrived.

I followed the sound of voices around the barn, where Kyle was talking with Honey and May near the hives. I'd seen the devastation from a distance yesterday, through the kitchen window, but nothing had prepared me for seeing it up close. Three wooden beehives sat in a neat row about fifty yards from the building, surrounded by an eerie silence. No buzzing. No movement. Just thousands of dark spots littering the ground.

Dead bees. Everywhere. A carpet of tiny bodies stretching out in all directions from the hives.

Yesterday, from inside the farmhouse, I'd seen dark shapes on the ground. But standing here now, close enough to smell the faint decay mixing with the perfume of nearby flowers, the scale of destruction was staggering.

Kyle spotted me and walked over, his expression professionally neutral even though I could see the tension in his shoulders. "Morning, Jessica. Thanks for coming."

I appreciated his use of my full name rather than "Jess," maintaining that professional distance with other officers around. "It's even worse up close. How many?"

"Honey estimates around 50,000 bees per hive. Three healthy colonies, completely destroyed."

A white pickup truck pulled into the drive behind me, and Kyle glanced over. "That'll be Dr. Fry now."

A man in his fifties with graying hair and wire-rimmed glasses climbed out, grabbing an equipment case from the truck bed. He wore jeans and a button-down shirt, and moved with the careful precision of someone used to detailed work.

"Dr. Neal Fry from the agricultural extension office," Kyle said quietly as the expert approached. "He's the bee expert."

Honey stood about ten feet away, her arms wrapped around herself. May was beside her, one hand on Honey's shoulder. Both women looked like they'd been crying.

Dr. Fry greeted Kyle with a handshake, then immediately got to work. He knelt near one of the hives, carefully placing something in a specimen container. The morning sun beat down on us, making the scene feel even more oppressive.

After several minutes of careful examination, Dr. Fry stood up and walked toward us, pulling off latex gloves. "I'm afraid I have some disturbing news," he said without preamble. "These bees weren't killed by disease or pesticide poisoning."

"What do you mean?" Honey's voice was barely a whisper.

"They were killed by Asian Giant Hornets. Vespa mandarinia. Also known as murder hornets."

The silence that followed was deafening. Even the breeze seemed to stop, as if the world itself was holding its breath.

"Murder hornets?" May's voice was sharp with disbelief. "But those aren't... they're not even native to this country. How is that possible?"

"You're right, they're not. They're from Asia. The only way they could be here is if someone deliberately introduced them." Dr. Fry's expression was stone serious. "Someone brought these hornets to your property specifically to destroy your hives."

Honey made a sound like she'd been punched in the stomach. May's hand tightened on her shoulder, though I noticed May's face remained strangely composed, her eyes scanning the area rather than focused on Honey's distress.

"How can you be sure?" Kyle asked, pulling out his notepad.

Dr. Fry walked back to the hives and picked up a small plastic container. Inside was what looked like a large wasp, easily two inches long with a distinctive yellow head and orange-striped abdomen. Even dead, it looked menacing.

"I found several dead hornets among the bees," Dr. Fry said, holding up the container. "The damage pattern is consistent with their attack method. They enter what's called a 'slaughter phase' where they decapitate the bees and take over the hive to feed on the larvae."

I felt sick. The heat of the morning sun suddenly felt oppressive, making the scene even more nightmarish.

"How long would it have taken?" I asked.

"A small group of these hornets can destroy a hive in a matter of hours. Based on what I'm seeing here, this happened fast. Probably sometime in the evening or early morning hours two days ago."

"But why would someone do this?" Honey's voice cracked. "Who would want to hurt my bees?"

Kyle and I exchanged a brief glance. We both knew about the suspicious customer who'd been asking detailed questions about Honey's operation.

"That's what we intend to find out," Kyle said. "Dr. Fry, is there any way to trace where these hornets came from?"

"Difficult, but not impossible. Someone would have had to acquire them through illegal channels. There are black market dealers who smuggle exotic insects, but it's risky and expensive." Dr. Fry sealed the container carefully. "Whoever did this had to know how to handle them safely. These hornets are aggressive, and their stings can be deadly to humans."

"Deadly?" May stepped back instinctively, her composure finally cracking.

"Their venom is highly toxic. Multiple stings can cause organ failure. And their stingers are long enough to penetrate most beekeeping suits." Dr. Fry gestured toward the area around the hives. "What's interesting is that they were all poisoned—looks like whoever released them also killed them afterward. Probably to prevent them from establishing a colony here or attacking anyone else. Asian Giant Hornets are a serious invasive species threat. If even a few survived and bred, we could have a major agricultural disaster on our hands. The fact that they were deliberately killed suggests the perpetrator understood the environmental risk and wanted to cover their tracks."

Honey shook her head helplessly. "I check the hives every morning, but I'm not out there all the time. The hives are behind the barn, out of sight from most of the property."

"What about security cameras?" Kyle asked.

"I never thought I'd need them. This is a quiet area. People respect each other's property." Honey's voice turned bitter. "Or so I thought."

Dr. Fry packed up his equipment. "I'll need to take some samples back to the lab for further analysis, but I'm confident in my preliminary findings. This was deliberate sabotage."

After Dr. Fry left, Kyle took statements from both Honey and May about the timeline and anyone they might have seen around the property. I waited by my car, watching the scene unfold. May pulled out her phone at one point, checking something before quickly putting it away. The gesture seemed oddly casual given the circumstances, though perhaps people dealt with shock in different ways.

When Kyle finished, Honey walked over to me, staring at the ruined hives with hollow eyes.

"I had those colonies for three years," Honey said quietly. "Built them up from nothing. Over 150,000 bees across the three hives, just... gone."

"Can you replace them?" I asked gently.

"Not this late in the season. And even if I could find bees for sale, I'd have to start over completely. New queens, new workers, rebuild the entire colony structure." Honey's shoulders sagged. "It takes months to establish a healthy hive. Maybe a year to get back to where I was."

"What about the bakery?" I asked.

"I can buy honey from other suppliers for now, but it won't be the same. My honey was part of what made the bakery special. People came specifically for products made with honey from my own bees." Honey gestured toward the rows of flowers visible in the distance, their bright colors seeming to mock the devastation. "And it's not just the honey. Those bees pollinated all my flowers. I sell cut flowers to the local florist and some shops in neighboring towns. Without the bees, the flower production will start declining too. It's all connected."

She looked at me with haunted eyes. "And without the farm income from both the honey and the flowers, I don't know how long I can keep the bakery open. The overhead, the employee costs..."

"Don't make any rash decisions," I said gently. "Give it some time."

"Time is exactly what I don't have." Honey's voice cracked, and I could see her fighting to hold back tears. "I'm sorry. I know you can't understand what this feels like. How could you possibly understand? To have everything you built just... destroyed."

The words hung in the air between us, and I felt my own throat tighten. She was right to think I couldn't understand. Most people couldn't. But I did. More than she knew.

I reached out and squeezed Honey's hand. "Actually, I do understand. More than you know."

Honey looked at me, surprised, her tear-filled eyes searching my face.

"When The Crock Pot opened, it was the best day of my life," I said quietly, the memories flooding back despite my efforts to keep them at bay. "I'd worked toward that moment for years. Everything was perfect. The dining room was packed, the food was excellent, the reviews were glowing." I paused, the memory still painful even a year later. "And then at the end of opening night, my sous chef Earl was murdered in the parking lot behind the restaurant."

Honey's hand tightened on mine. "I remember hearing about that. It was all over the news. I'm so sorry, Jess."

"The next few weeks were hell. The restaurant became a spectacle. People came in droves, but half of them just wanted to gawk at where it happened, ask morbid questions. I couldn't sleep. I couldn't eat. I kept thinking I should just close the doors, sell the equipment, give up." I met her eyes. "But I didn't. I kept going. One day at a time. And eventually, things got better. The curiosity seekers moved on, and real customers stayed."

"How long did it take?" Honey asked, her voice small.

"For business to recover? About three months. For me to stop having nightmares?" I swallowed hard. "I still have them sometimes. But they're less frequent now."

"Three months," Honey repeated, looking back at her dead hives. "I don't know if I can make it three months without the farm income."

"You might be surprised at what you can survive when you have to," I said. "And you're not alone. Shayla needs this job. The community loves your bakery. We'll figure something out."

Honey nodded, but I could see the doubt in her eyes. She was looking at the worst-case scenario, and right now, it probably felt inevitable.

May approached us, her face set in determined lines. "Honey, we need to talk about Clark Marlowe's offer. He said it's still good."

I felt my jaw tighten at the mention of Clark's name. I remembered him showing up at the farm on Tuesday, barely a day after the bees had died, already circling with his offer. The man had no shame.

"May, not now," Honey said, her voice weary.

"When, then? When we're bankrupt? When we've lost everything?" May's voice took on an edge. "We need to be realistic. Without the bees, we can't sustain both the farm and the bakery. If we sell the land to Clark now, we can at least walk away with something."

I thought back to just two days ago, when May had stood in Honey's kitchen and declared, "We'll rebuild. We won't let whoever did this win." What had changed? Was it the confirmation that this was deliberate sabotage? Or had she been thinking about selling all along?

"I'm not selling to Clark Marlowe." Honey's voice was firm despite the tears still glistening in her eyes.

"Why not? He's offering good money. More than fair market value."

"Because this land has been in my family for three generations. My grandmother built this farm. My mother expanded it. I'm not going to be the one who sells it off to some developer just because things got hard."

"Things didn't just 'get hard,' Honey. Someone destroyed your business. On purpose. What if they come back? What if they do something worse?" May's concern seemed genuine, though something about the timing of raising this issue bothered me.

"Then I'll deal with it when it happens. But I'm not making decisions based on fear."

"I'm not asking you to make decisions based on fear. I'm asking you to make them based on reality. We can't keep the farm going without bees. You said it yourself, it'll take months, maybe a year to rebuild the colonies. Do we have that kind of time?"

"I don't know," Honey admitted. "But I know I'm not ready to give up yet."

"I'm not saying give up. I'm saying be smart. Take the money while it's on the table. Start fresh somewhere else. Maybe open a bakery that doesn't depend on a farm."

"The farm is part of what makes the bakery special," Honey insisted. "People know the honey comes from my own bees. That's the whole point."

"The point is to survive," May said. "And right now, survival means considering all our options."

"I'm not going to let fear drive me out of my own business," Honey said firmly.

May looked like she wanted to argue more, but Kyle's approach interrupted them.

Kyle walked over to us, maintaining that professional demeanor. "Honey, I'm going to need you to think hard about anyone who's shown unusual interest in your operation. The person Shayla described sounds like a good lead, but there might be others."

"I'll try. My head isn't very clear right now."

"I understand. Just call me if anything comes to mind." Kyle turned to me. "Ms. Vasquez, can I talk to you for a minute?"

We walked a few steps away from the others, and only then did his shoulders relax slightly, his voice dropping to a more familiar tone.

"This wasn't random," Kyle said quietly. "Someone specifically targeted Honey's business. The question is why."

"Maybe someone wanted to buy her land," I said, thinking of Clark Marlowe's convenient offer that was "still good."

"Or eliminate competition," Kyle added. "We'll look into both angles."

"Kyle, did you notice May's reaction back there?"

"What about it?"

"She seemed more concerned about the financial implications than the actual destruction. And she brought up Clark Marlowe's offer almost immediately. Like she'd been thinking about it already. Two days ago, she was saying they'd rebuild and not let whoever did this win. Now she's pushing to sell."

Kyle's expression turned thoughtful. "That's interesting. I noticed she was checking her phone during the investigation. Seemed out of place."

"Vee mentioned last night that we should look at who benefits from the farm failing. May is a partner. If they can't recover and have to sell..."

"She'd get her forty-nine percent of the sale price," Kyle finished. "I'll look into their partnership agreement. See what the terms are."

"Be careful how you approach her. If she is involved, we don't want to tip her off."

"Always careful." Kyle's expression softened for just a moment, his professional mask slipping. "You heading home?"

"Yeah. I need to process all this. And I should probably check in at the restaurant."

"Drive safe. I'll call you later."

I walked back to my car, giving Honey one last reassuring hug before I left. As I pulled out of the gravel drive, I could see May in my rearview mirror, standing alone by the hives, phone in hand again.

The drive back to town gave me too much time to think. My mind kept returning to those thousands of dead bees scattered around the hives like a carpet of death. Someone had planned this attack carefully, acquired dangerous exotic insects, and carried out the destruction with cold precision.

But it wasn't just the planning that bothered me. It was the cruelty of it. Whoever did this didn't just want to hurt Honey's business. They wanted to destroy something she loved, something she'd built with her own hands over years of careful work.

The memory of Earl's murder surfaced again, unbidden. Finding him behind the dumpster on opening night. The way his death had nearly destroyed me, nearly destroyed The Crock Pot before it even had a chance to thrive. But I'd had support. My friends, my family, even my difficult mother had rallied around me in those first terrible days.

Honey had May, but after today's observations, I wasn't sure May was the support Honey needed. The quick focus on finances, the immediate suggestion to sell. It felt off, even if I couldn't quite put my finger on why.

My phone rang through the car's Bluetooth. Vee's name appeared on the screen.

"Hey," I answered.

"How did it go? What did the expert say?"

"Asian Giant Hornets. Murder hornets. Someone deliberately introduced them to destroy Honey's hives."

"Oh my God. That's... that's psychotic."

"Yeah. And Vee, I think you might be right to question May. Something's off about her."

"What do you mean?"

I filled her in on May's behavior at the farm, her immediate focus on finances, her suggestion about Clark Marlowe's offer, the phone checking, the controlled demeanor while Honey fell apart.

"That's suspicious," Vee said. "Very suspicious."

"Kyle's looking into their partnership agreement. But I keep thinking about what you said last night. About who benefits if the farm fails."

"And May benefits. Big time. She gets out of a struggling business and walks away with money from the land sale."

"Exactly. But would she really kill 150,000 bees just to force a sale?"

"People have done worse for money," Vee said darkly. "Remember Zane from the Garrett Majors case? He killed Garrett because he felt disrespected and undervalued. Sometimes people snap when they feel trapped."

I shuddered at the memory. Zane had seemed so normal, so harmless, until he wasn't. "True. But this feels different somehow. More calculated."

"Or maybe that's what they want you to think. Maybe the calculated approach is exactly what makes it so dangerous."

"Maybe." I pulled into The Crock Pot's parking lot. "I'm at the restaurant. I need to check in with Noah."

"Okay. But Jess? Be careful. If May is involved, and if she figures out you're suspicious of her..."

"I know. I will be."

After hanging up, I sat in my car for a moment, staring at the restaurant. The familiar sight of the building usually brought me comfort, but today all I could think about was Earl. About loss. About how quickly something you loved could be taken away.

I thought about what I'd told Honey. About Earl, about keeping going one day at a time, about not giving up.

I'd meant every word. But I'd also learned something important from Earl's murder: sometimes the people closest to you are the ones you should watch most carefully. And right now, May Lowen was looking very suspicious indeed.

The question was: who hated Honey enough to destroy everything she'd worked for? Or more accurately, who stood to gain enough to be willing to commit such a cruel act?

I pulled out my phone and texted Vee: We need to update the murder board tonight. Lots of new information.

Vee's response came immediately: Already planning on it. This is getting serious.

Very serious, I typed back. And possibly very dangerous.

I got out of the car and headed into the restaurant, my mind already working through suspects, motives, and opportunities. Someone had planned this attack for weeks, maybe months. They'd acquired illegal insects, learned how to handle them safely, and executed their plan with precision.

That level of calculation wasn't random. It was personal, financial, or both.

And I was determined to figure out which one it was before someone got hurt. Because if those hornets could kill 150,000 bees in a matter of hours, what else might they be capable of? And more importantly, if May's concern about "something worse" was genuine, what would the perpetrator do next?

Chapter Six

After a quick check-in with Noah at The Crock Pot, where he assured me everything was under control, I drove over to Honey's Sweet Treats. The bakery sat on Main Street, wedged between a used bookstore and a vintage clothing shop. The cheerful yellow awning and hand-painted sign seemed almost mockingly bright given what had happened.

The bell above the door chimed as I entered. The smell of fresh bread and cinnamon immediately enveloped me, and for a moment I could almost forget the devastation I'd witnessed that morning.

"Jess!" Shayla looked up from behind the counter, relief flooding her face. "How did it go? What did the expert say?"

I glanced around the bakery. Two elderly women sat at a small table near the window, sharing a coffee cake. A man in coveralls stood at the counter, apparently deciding between muffin flavors.

"Can we talk in a minute?" I asked quietly.

Shayla nodded, finishing up with the customer. "The blueberry muffins are really good today, Mr. Peterson."

"I'll take two then, and one of those bear claws for my wife."

After he left, the two older women approached the counter.

"Shayla, dear," one of them said, "we heard about poor Honey's bees. Such a terrible thing. Is she doing alright?"

"She's devastated, Mrs. Talbot. But she's trying to stay strong."

"Well, you tell her that Harold and I are praying for her. And if there's anything we can do..." The woman trailed off, shaking her head. "Who would do such a thing to innocent creatures?"

"Thank you. I'll tell her."

After the women left, Shayla flipped the sign to "Back in 15 Minutes" and locked the door.

"Okay, tell me everything."

I filled her in on Dr. Fry's findings, watching Shayla's face grow paler with each detail.

"Asian Giant Hornets? Someone brought them here on purpose?" Shayla sank into one of the chairs. "That's... that's psychotic."

"It gets worse. They're calling it deliberate sabotage. Someone planned this, Shay. They researched how to destroy Honey's business and then they did it."

"But why? Honey's the sweetest person in the world. She pays me fairly, she's flexible with my schedule because of the twins, she's even teaching me her grandmother's cake recipes." Shayla's voice cracked. "Who could hate her enough to do this?"

"That's what we need to figure out." I sat down across from her. "You mentioned that suspicious customer a few weeks ago. Can you think of anyone else who's been asking unusual questions? Or seemed too interested in Honey's operation?"

Shayla was quiet for a moment, thinking. "Actually, yes. There was this woman who came in about a month ago. She ordered a dozen cupcakes, but she spent most of the time asking about our suppliers. Wanted to know where we got our honey, our flour, our eggs. Said she was thinking of opening her own bakery."

"What did she look like?"

"Blonde, maybe forty-something. Really put together, you know? Expensive clothes, perfect makeup. She had this way of talking that made it sound like she was being friendly, but her questions felt... calculating."

I felt a chill. "Did she say what kind of bakery she wanted to open?"

"She said she and her husband were considering it. Something about bringing 'elevated desserts' to the area." Shayla made air quotes. "Like our desserts weren't good enough."

"Do you remember her name?"

"She paid with a credit card. Let me check." Shayla went behind the counter and pulled out a small notebook where she recorded daily sales. "Here it is. Abby Douglas."

My pulse quickened. Dale and Abby Douglas. The couple who owned the competing bakery that couldn't quite get traction.

"Shayla, I think I need to pay a visit to Dreamy Desserts."

"The bakery over on Oak Street? Why?"

"Just a hunch. Be careful while I'm gone, okay? And call me if anyone comes by asking strange questions."

Twenty minutes later, I stood outside Dreamy Desserts. The bakery was smaller than Honey's, with a more modern aesthetic.

Clean lines, minimalist décor, and a display case filled with elaborate pastries that looked almost too perfect to eat.

The contrast with Honey's cozy, homey atmosphere was stark.

The bell chimed as I stepped inside. Behind the counter stood a blonde woman who matched Shayla's description perfectly. She looked up with a practiced smile that didn't quite reach her eyes.

"Welcome to Dreamy Desserts. I'm Abby. How can I help you today?"

"Hi, I'm Jessica Vasquez. I own The Crock Pot restaurant."

"Oh, of course! I've heard wonderful things about your place. We've been meaning to stop by." She gestured toward the display case. "Can I get you something? Our croissants are fresh this morning."

I glanced around while she talked, taking in the details. The bakery was beautiful, no question about that. Sleek marble countertops, pendant lighting that probably cost more than my monthly restaurant supply budget, and a gleaming espresso machine that looked like it belonged in an upscale Italian café.

But there were also telltale signs of struggle. Only two small tables, both empty. The display case, while filled with gorgeous pastries, had items that looked like they'd been sitting for a while. The edges of some croissants were getting hard, and a few tarts had that slightly dried-out look that came from being under heat lamps too long.

More tellingly, there were no customers. At eleven o'clock on a weekday morning, a successful bakery should have at least some traffic. Honey's place had been bustling when I left. This place felt like a museum, beautiful but lifeless.

The place smelled amazing, vanilla and butter and chocolate, but there was a desperate quality to the perfection. Like they were trying too hard to be something they weren't.

"Actually, I wanted to talk to you about Honey Jacobson," I said. "I heard about what happened to her bees."

Abby's expression shifted slightly, becoming more guarded. "Terrible thing. Such a shame."

"You know Honey well?"

"We're... competitors, I suppose you could say. Though we serve different markets." Abby gestured to her display case. "We focus more on artisanal desserts, European techniques. A more sophisticated palate."

As she gestured, my eyes followed the movement and caught a stack of papers partially hidden under the cash register. The top one, from a commercial kitchen supply company, had "FINAL NOTICE" stamped in red across the top.

There was something dismissive in her tone that rubbed me the wrong way.

"I understand you visited her bakery recently. Asked about her suppliers?"

Now Abby's smile faltered completely. "I'm sorry, who did you say you were again?"

"Jessica Vasquez. I'm a friend of Honey's."

"Right. Well, I may have stopped by. It's common courtesy to introduce yourself to other business owners in the area."

"Of course. And your husband? Is he here? I'd love to meet him too."

"Dale's in the back. But we're actually quite busy today, so..."

Just then, a man emerged from the kitchen area. He was tall and thin, with thinning brown hair and nervous energy. He wiped his hands on his apron and looked questioningly at his wife.

"Dale, this is Jessica from The Crock Pot. She was just asking about our visit to Honey's place."

Dale's eyes darted between his wife and me. "Oh. Yes. Terrible what happened to those bees."

"It really is," I said. "I don't know much about beekeeping, but I've been reading about it. Apparently the hive structure is incredibly complex."

"The social organization is fascinating," Dale said, his nervous energy seeming to ease slightly as he talked. "The way the queen controls everything, how the workers know their roles instinctively. It's like a perfectly organized society."

I tilted my head, surprised. "You sound like you know a lot about it."

Dale's face flushed. "What? No, I just... I mean, doesn't everyone find that stuff interesting?" He glanced at Abby, who was giving him an odd look. "I probably saw a documentary or something."

"Right," I said slowly, filing the observation away. It seemed like an unusually detailed knowledge for someone who'd just "seen a documentary," but maybe he was just one of those people who retained random facts.

"Especially since someone did it on purpose," I said, watching their reactions carefully.

Abby's face went pale. "On purpose?"

"The expert confirmed it this morning. Someone deliberately introduced Asian Giant Hornets to destroy her colonies."

"That's... that's horrible," Dale stammered, but his eyes darted to Abby with an expression I couldn't quite read. Fear? Warning?

Abby's hand gripped the edge of the counter, her knuckles going white. "I don't understand. Who would do something like that?"

"That's what the police are trying to figure out." I watched them carefully. Dale had taken a step back toward the kitchen, as if considering escape. Abby's jaw was clenched so tight a muscle twitched in her cheek. "They're looking at anyone who might benefit from Honey's bakery failing."

"We had nothing to do with that," Abby said quickly. Too quickly. "We barely know Honey."

"But you did visit her bakery. Asked detailed questions about her suppliers, her operation."

"That's just good business practice," Abby shot back, her voice rising slightly. "Researching the competition."

"Of course." I pulled out my phone and pretended to check a message. "The police will probably want to verify everyone's whereabouts for the night the hornets were released. Two nights ago, evening hours."

Dale made a small sound, almost a whimper. Abby shot him a look that could have frozen fire.

"We were here," Abby said firmly. "Working late. We're here most nights, trying to build our business."

"Can anyone verify that?"

"We were alone. It was just the two of us."

"Right." I tucked my phone away. "Well, I should get going. I'm sure the police will be in touch."

Dale's hand was shaking as he gripped the doorframe to the kitchen. A bead of sweat ran down his temple despite the air-conditioned coolness of the shop.

"Wait," Abby called out as I reached for the door handle. "Why are you here? Why are you asking us these questions?"

I turned back. "Like I said, I'm a friend of Honey's. And I don't like seeing good people hurt by whoever did this."

"Neither do we," Abby said, but there was something brittle in her voice.

I headed for the door, then paused. "Oh, and congratulations."

"For what?" Abby asked, her voice tight.

"Well, with Honey's bakery struggling, I imagine you'll finally get the traction you've been looking for."

The silence behind me was deafening. Dale looked like he might be sick. Abby's face had gone from pale to flushed, her hands balled into fists at her sides.

"Get out," Abby said quietly.

"Excuse me?"

"I said get out. We don't have to answer your questions. You're not the police."

"You're right. I'm not." I opened the door, the bell chiming cheerfully. "But they will be coming. And when they do, I hope you have better answers than you gave me."

I sat in my car for a moment, my heart pounding. That had been more confrontational than I'd intended, but their reactions had been so clearly guilty of something. The question was what.

I pulled out my phone and called Kyle.

"Hey," he answered on the second ring. "Everything okay?"

"I just left Dreamy Desserts. Kyle, you need to talk to Dale and Abby Douglas."

"The competing bakery owners?"

"Yes. I went there to ask some casual questions about Honey, and they completely fell apart. Abby went pale when I mentioned the deliberate sabotage, Dale looked like he was going to be sick, and when I asked where they were two nights ago, they claimed they were alone at the bakery with no one to verify."

"Jess." Kyle's tone was a mixture of exasperation and concern. "You can't just go interrogating suspects."

"I wasn't interrogating. I was shopping for pastries and making conversation."

"Did you buy any pastries?"

"That's beside the point. Kyle, something is very wrong there. Their bakery is gorgeous but completely empty. Not a single customer the whole time I was there. I saw final notice bills under the register. And the way they looked at each other when I mentioned the hornets, it was like they were communicating without words."

I heard him sigh. "What exactly did you say to them?"

"I told them the expert confirmed deliberate sabotage. I mentioned the police would want to verify everyone's whereabouts. And I may have congratulated them on finally getting the traction they've been looking for with Honey out of the picture."

"Jess."

"I know, I know. But Kyle, you should have seen their faces. Dale was shaking. Abby kicked me out when I pushed too hard."

"She kicked you out?"

"Told me to leave. Said I wasn't the police and they didn't have to answer my questions."

Kyle was quiet for a moment. "Alright. I'll go talk to them this afternoon. But Jess, you need to back off. If they are involved, you just put yourself on their radar."

"I'm already on someone's radar. Might as well make sure it's the right someone."

"That's not funny. This person used deadly insects. They're dangerous."

"I know. But so am I when someone threatens people I care about." I started my car. "Will you call me after you talk to them?"

"Yes. Where are you heading now?"

"Home. I need to pick up the twins later and I've got some things to do before then."

"Good. Stay around people. Don't go anywhere alone."

"Kyle—"

"I mean it, Jess. Promise me."

I heard the fear underlying his professional tone. "I promise. I'll be careful."

"Thank you. I'll call you later."

After hanging up, I sat for another moment, replaying the conversation with Dale and Abby. Their nervousness. Their lack of alibi. The final notice bills. The empty bakery that must be hemorrhaging money.

I pulled up my text thread with Vee and typed: **Just left Dreamy Desserts. Dale and Abby Douglas are definitely hiding something. Adding them to the suspect list tonight when we update the board.**

Vee's response came quickly: **What did you do?**

Nothing! Just asked some questions.

Jess...

Okay, I may have rattled their cages a bit. But they practically confessed just by their reactions.

Be CAREFUL. These people might be dangerous.

Everyone keeps telling me that. I'm starting to think I should be worried.

You SHOULD be worried. That's my point.

I smiled despite the tension. **Love you too. See you tonight.**

I put my phone away and pulled out of the parking spot. As I drove toward home, I noticed a dark pickup truck a few cars back. It stayed behind me through two turns, maintaining the same distance.

My hands tightened on the steering wheel. Was I being paranoid, or was someone following me?

I made a sudden turn down a side street. The truck continued straight.

I let out a breath I didn't know I'd been holding. Just paranoia. But maybe everyone was right. Maybe I should be more careful.

Because whoever killed Honey's bees had planned it for weeks, had acquired illegal insects, and had executed their attack with cold precision. That wasn't someone who would take kindly to a nosy restaurant owner asking uncomfortable questions.

But I had never been good at backing down when people I cared about were threatened. And right now, Honey, Shayla, and the twins all depended on that bakery staying open.

Which meant I wasn't backing down. Not yet.

Chapter Seven

The drive to Pinehurst had become one of my favorite parts of the week, even if it meant navigating thirty minutes of highway traffic each direction. Wednesday therapy appointments gave me uninterrupted time with the twins, no restaurant stress, no murder investigations, just the three of us.

"How was school today?" I asked as Ivy and Dove climbed into the backseat.

"Good! We learned about fractions!" Dove announced.

"And I got an A on my spelling test," Ivy added proudly.

"That's fantastic. You've both been working so hard."

The drive was filled with their usual chatter about friends, teachers, and plans for Riley and Sawyer's baby shower. I found their excitement infectious. After everything they'd been through, seeing them plan a party with the pure joy of eight-year-olds felt like a small miracle.

I dropped them off at Dr. Martinez's office and settled into the waiting room with my phone. Kyle had texted earlier asking about dinner plans.

Kyle: Want to do dinner tonight? I'm thinking Sushi 73 around 6?

Me: Perfect! The twins will love that. Should we meet you there?

Kyle: Sounds good. I'll grab us a table.

Me: See you at 6.

An hour later, the twins emerged from their session, both looking relaxed and happy. Dr. Martinez gave me a wave, gesturing for me to step into the office.

"They're doing remarkably well," Dr. Martinez said. "Very resilient kids. Do you have a minute? I'd like to show you something."

I followed her into the small, warmly decorated office. Dr. Martinez was in her fifties, with kind eyes and an easy manner that had helped the twins open up from their very first session.

"The girls have been doing art therapy with me," Dr. Martinez said, pulling out a folder. "And I think you'll find their recent work very encouraging."

She laid out two drawings on her desk. The first one made my throat tight with emotion. It showed five stick figures, clearly labeled in Ivy's careful handwriting: "Jess," "Vee," "Shayla," "Me" (with an arrow pointing to a figure with Ivy's signature pink backpack), and "Dove" (with a purple backpack). At their feet were two cats, one gray and white, one black and white, labeled "Lulu" and "Baxter."

They were all holding hands in front of a house with a bright yellow sun overhead. Hearts floated around the figures.

"This is their family portrait," Dr. Martinez explained. "What's significant here is that they've included everyone in the household, including the cats. The way they're holding hands, the hearts, the bright sun, these all indicate feelings of security and belonging."

"They drew this today?" I asked, my voice thick.

"Last week, actually. But they've been expanding on it in each session. Look." Dr. Martinez pointed to small details. "Ivy added the garden behind the house in our session two weeks ago. Dove added the butterflies last week. They're building a sense of home, Jess. That's huge progress."

I blinked back tears. After everything the twins had been through, losing their mother to murder, being placed with their grandmother who turned out to be involved in the killing, the trauma of being held hostage, seeing them create something so hopeful felt like a miracle.

"And this one?" I asked, pointing to the second drawing.

This one was more complex. It showed the same house, but the sky was darker, filled with storm clouds. Rain fell in heavy lines. But in the foreground, bright flowers bloomed, daisies, sunflowers, roses. Butterflies in vibrant colors flew among the flowers, and a rainbow arced across one corner of the page, partially obscured by the clouds.

"This is Dove's," Dr. Martinez said. "And it's actually very healthy."

"It looks sad."

"It looks honest," Dr. Martinez corrected gently. "Dove is acknowledging that bad things have happened. The storms, the darkness, that's real. But look at what she's chosen to put in the foreground. The flowers are bigger than the house. The butterflies are everywhere. And that rainbow? She told me that's what comes after storms."

I felt tears spill over. "She said that?"

"She did. She's processing her trauma in a very mature way. She's not pretending the bad things didn't happen, but she's also not letting them define her entire world. The flowers and butterflies represent growth, transformation, hope."

"What about Ivy? Did she draw something like this too?"

Dr. Martinez pulled out another drawing, similar but with Ivy's distinctive style. Her storms were more abstract, swirls of dark colors, but the flowers were more detailed, each petal carefully colored. A large butterfly dominated the center, its wings spanning almost the entire page.

"Ivy's approach is slightly different," Dr. Martinez explained. "She's more focused on the transformation aspect. See how the butterfly is emerging from the darkness? She told me it's learning to fly even though there are still storms."

"They're so much braver than I am," I whispered.

"They feel safe with you," Dr. Martinez said. "That's why they can process this. Children can't heal from trauma if they don't feel secure in their present. You, Vee, and Shayla have given them that security. This artwork is evidence of that."

"What do I do with these?"

"I'd like to keep them in their files for now, but I wanted you to see them. To understand what's happening in their therapy." Dr. Martinez smiled. "They're doing the work, Jess. They're healing. And that's because of the environment you've created for them."

I nodded, unable to speak. I looked at the drawings again, the bright family portrait, and the storm pictures with their defiant flowers and hopeful butterflies.

"Thank you," I finally managed. "For showing me this. For helping them."

"It's my privilege. They're remarkable children." Dr. Martinez collected the drawings and tucked them back into the folder. "Same time next week?"

"Absolutely."

As I walked back to the waiting room, I felt lighter despite the emotion. The twins were healing. They were building a life, a family, a sense of home. And somehow, in the middle of investigating bee murders and dodging potential threats, I'd helped create something beautiful for two little girls who'd seen too much darkness.

The twins looked up as I entered, both smiling. Dove was showing Ivy something on the waiting room's toy shelf, their heads together in that way that only twins had.

"Ready to go?" I asked.

"Can we get ice cream on the way home?" Ivy asked hopefully.

"It's Wednesday," Dove added. "Ice Cream Wednesday."

I laughed. We'd started that tradition months ago, and the twins never let me forget. "Ice Cream Wednesday it is. And then we're meeting Kyle for dinner at Sushi 73."

"Yay!" both girls cheered. "Can we get California rolls?"

"You can get whatever you want."

The drive home was quieter after our ice cream stop, both girls tired from their session. They perked up when I reminded them about dinner with Kyle.

"Will he tell us police stories?" Dove asked.

"If you ask nicely, he might."

"Can we ask about the bad guy who hurt the bees?" Ivy wondered.

I hesitated, glancing at the girls in my rearview mirror. After everything the twins had been through, I was trying to be more careful about what we discussed around them. "Maybe we should stick to other police stories tonight. Happier ones."

By the time we got home, it was almost five o'clock. Vee and Shayla were both already there, changed out of their work clothes.

"How did therapy go?" Shayla asked.

"Great. Dr. Martinez says they're doing really well." I ruffled Ivy's hair. "And we're all going to Sushi 73 to meet Kyle for dinner at six."

"Ooh, I love Sushi 73!" Vee said. "Let me change into something cuter."

"Me too," Shayla added, heading toward her room.

The twins ran to their room to change out of their school clothes, leaving me a few minutes to text Kyle.

Me: Everyone's excited. We should all be there right at 6.

Kyle: Perfect. Can't wait to see you all.

At five forty-five, we piled into my car and headed to Sushi 73. The restaurant was on Main Street with its distinctive glass and neon facade glowing in the early evening light. Even from the parking lot, I could see the colorful neon signs that made the place look modern and sleek.

"I love this place," Ivy said as we walked across the lot.

"Me too. Chef Kano makes the best sushi," Dove added.

Through the large front windows, I could see Kyle already seated at a table near the window. He must have spotted us too, because he lifted his hand in a wave. The twins waved back enthusiastically.

We stepped through the glass doors into the bright, modern interior. The restaurant was busy but not packed, with maybe half the tables occupied. The all-glass counter ran along one side, where Chef Kano stood behind it, expertly slicing a roll into perfect pieces.

"Jess!" he yelled, his booming voice carrying across the restaurant. He looked up from his work with a huge grin. "Welcome, welcome! And you brought the whole crew!"

I couldn't help but smile. Kano was always like this, loud and welcoming and genuine. He wore his chef's whites with a colorful bandana tied around his head, his usual style.

"Hey, Kano. Good to see you."

"And look at these two!" He gestured at the twins with his knife. "Getting so big! What are you now, ten?"

"Eight!" both girls corrected, giggling.

"Eight? No way. I don't believe it." He winked at them, then his eyes swept over Vee and Shayla. "Vee, Shayla, good to see you both. It's been too long!"

"Hey, Kano," Vee said with a wave.

Suzy, Kano's wife, appeared from the back carrying a tray of drinks. She was petite with a warm smile, her dark hair pulled back in a neat ponytail. When she saw us, her face lit up.

"Oh, my goodness, the Vasquez crew!" She set the tray down at another table and came over to give me a quick hug. "How have you been, Jess? We haven't seen you in weeks!"

"I know, I've been swamped at the restaurant. But we're here now."

"Bringing the whole family tonight, I see!" Kano called from behind the counter, his eyes twinkling with mischief. "Got your officer waiting at the window table and everything. Should I start practicing my wedding toast?"

I felt my cheeks warm despite the bright neon lights doing their best to hide it. "Kano, please."

"What? I'm just saying, it's good to see you so happy, Jess. This is what you deserve," he said, his tone softening into something genuine.

"Leave her alone," Suzy swatted at him playfully with her order pad. "Come on, I'll take you to your table."

"Kyle!" the twins suddenly shouted and took off running across the restaurant.

Kyle stood up as they approached, catching them both in hugs. "Hey, you two! How was therapy?"

"Good!" they said in unison.

"I want to sit next to you!" Ivy announced.

"No, I do!" Dove protested.

The rest of us caught up to find Kyle laughing at their competing claims. "Okay, okay. How about this?" He moved to a different seat at the table. "See? Now I have a spot on each side. Ivy on my left, Dove on my right. Problem solved."

Both girls beamed and quickly claimed their spots on either side of him.

"Smart man," Vee said with a grin as we all settled into our seats.

"I've learned a thing or two about negotiation," Kyle said, winking at the twins.

"Can I start you all with drinks?" Suzy asked, pulling out her order pad.

"Green tea for me," I said.

"Same," Kyle added.

"Can we get Shirley Temples?" Dove asked hopefully.

"With extra cherries?" Ivy added.

"Of course, sweethearts." Suzy wrote it down. "Vee? Shayla?"

"I'll have a Coke," Vee said.

"Same for me," Shayla added.

"Perfect. I'll get those right out, and you all take your time with the menu." Suzy headed back toward the counter.

"So," Kyle said, looking at the twins on either side of him, "how was school today?"

"Good! I got an A on my spelling test," Ivy announced proudly.

"That's fantastic," Kyle said. "What words were on the test?"

As Ivy started listing her spelling words, I caught Kano watching us from behind the counter. He gave me a thumbs up and a wink before going back to his work. I shook my head, trying not to laugh.

"What?" Kyle asked, noticing my expression.

"Nothing. Kano's just being Kano."

Kyle grinned. "The wedding toast comment?"

"You heard that?"

"The whole restaurant heard that. He's not exactly subtle."

Vee laughed. "That's putting it mildly."

Before I could respond, Suzy returned with our drinks, including the twins' Shirley Temples complete with three cherries each.

"Are we ready to order, or do you need a few more minutes?" she asked.

"I think we're ready," I said, looking around the table. Everyone nodded.

The twins ordered their usual California rolls and edamame. Vee got the teriyaki chicken bowl. Shayla chose the spicy salmon roll. Kyle ordered the unagi avocado roll, and I went with my favorite, the spicy tuna bowl.

"Excellent choices," Suzy said, writing everything down. "This should be out in about fifteen minutes. Kano will start on it right away."

As she walked away, Kyle leaned back in his chair, careful not to jostle the twins on either side. "So, therapy went well today?"

"Really well," I said, keeping my voice low enough that the twins, who were now coloring on the paper placemats with the crayons Suzy had brought, wouldn't hear the details. "Dr. Martinez showed me some of their artwork. They're processing everything in really healthy ways."

"That's great to hear." Kyle's expression softened. "They're strong kids."

"They are. But they've had to be."

Shayla jumped into the conversation. "Honey seemed better today at the bakery too. She's starting to talk about rebuilding plans."

"That's good," Kyle said. "Any updates on the investigation from your end?"

"Nothing concrete yet," I admitted. "But I'm keeping my eyes and ears open."

"Well, can you maybe keep your eyes and ears open without getting into dangerous situations?" Kyle asked, his tone light but with an undertone of seriousness.

"I'm always careful."

"Jess," Vee said, giving me a look. "You are many wonderful things, but 'always careful' is not one of them."

Before I could defend myself, Kano's voice boomed across the restaurant. "Jess! I forgot to tell you. I tried that new soup recipe you posted on your Instagram. The roasted red pepper and tomato?"

"Yeah? How'd it turn out?"

"Fantastic! My wife couldn't stop eating it. You've got to teach me that trick you do with the cream at the end."

"It's all about the temperature when you add it," I called back. "Too hot and it breaks."

"That's what I figured. Next time you're here, we'll trade secrets. I'll show you my new roll technique if you show me that soup trick."

"Deal!"

Kyle watched this exchange with an amused smile. "You two are like competitive siblings."

"That's exactly what we are," I said. "Ever since that hometown competition where he beat me."

"And I'll never let her forget it!" Kano shouted, clearly eavesdropping on our conversation.

"You won one competition!" I shouted back.

"The most important one!"

Everyone at our table laughed, and I noticed other diners smiling at the banter. This was normal for Sushi 73. Kano was always like this, loud and friendly and making everyone feel like family.

Suzy appeared with our food, placing each dish carefully in front of us. "Here you go. Kano made Jess's spicy tuna bowl extra special tonight."

I looked down at my bowl. It was perfect, just the way Kano always made it for me, with extra avocado and the spicy mayo drizzled in my favorite pattern.

"Tell him thank you," I said to Suzy.

"Tell him yourself. He's waiting to hear what you think."

I looked up to see Kano watching from behind the counter. I gave him two thumbs up, and he grinned, returning to his work.

"He really knows what you like," Kyle observed, starting on his unagi roll.

"We've known each other for years. He comes into The Crock Pot all the time too. Always orders alphabet soup with half a turkey club."

"It's so good," Kano called out. He was definitely still listening to every word we said. "Best soup in town!"

"Thank you!" I called back.

Dinner was easy and comfortable. The twins told Kyle about their upcoming butterfly project presentation, fighting over who got to tell which part of the story. Vee shared stories from her mail route. Shayla talked about the new honey cake recipe she and Honey were working on. Kyle told us about a K-9 demonstration he'd helped with at the elementary school earlier in the week.

It felt normal. Natural. Like this was something we did all the time, not just a special occasion.

Halfway through dinner, a family at another table waved at me. I recognized them as regular customers from The Crock Pot.

"Chef Jessica! Great to see you!" the dad called.

"You too! Thanks for coming in last week."

"The meatloaf special was incredible."

"Glad you enjoyed it!"

This was Dashwood. Everyone knew everyone, and seeing familiar faces everywhere you went was just part of life here. I loved it.

By the time we finished eating, the twins were getting sleepy, both leaning against Kyle from either side. He had his arms around both of them, talking quietly about something that made them giggle.

Kyle picked up the check before I could reach for it.

"My treat," he said firmly.

"Kyle, you don't have to do that."

"I know I don't have to. I want to."

We gathered our things and headed to the counter where Suzy was waiting with the bill. Kyle paid while I said goodbye to Kano.

"Thanks for dinner, Kano. It was perfect as always."

"Anytime, Jess. And hey," he leaned over the counter, lowering his voice slightly, "I wasn't joking earlier. You really do deserve this. All of it."

My throat tightened unexpectedly. "Thanks, Kano."

He straightened up, his usual booming voice returning. "Now get out of here before I start getting sentimental! See you all next time!"

"Bye, Chef Kano!" the twins called.

"Bye, girls! Study hard in school!"

We filed out into the parking lot, the cool evening air a nice contrast to the warm restaurant. The twins were definitely fading, both yawning as we walked to the car.

"That was really nice," Vee said. "We should do that more often."

"Definitely," Shayla agreed.

Kyle walked us to my car. "Drive safe. Text me when you get home?"

"I will."

He gave me a quick hug, then leaned down to the twins' level. "See you girls soon, okay?"

"Bye, Kyle," they said in unison, already half-asleep.

On the drive home, the twins fell asleep in the backseat almost immediately. Vee rode shotgun while Shayla sat in back with the girls, gently moving Dove's head to rest more comfortably against her shoulder.

Tonight had been good. Really good. Not just the food or the company, but the feeling of normalcy. Of family. Of having people who cared about us, like Kano and Suzy, who'd known me for years and still treated me like I mattered.

After everything with the investigation, the threats, the worry about Honey and the bakery, tonight had been exactly what I needed.

A reminder that life was more than just solving crimes and catching bad guys.

It was also about spicy tuna bowls and Shirley Temples with extra cherries. About friendly rivalries and inside jokes. About the twins falling asleep in the backseat and Vee humming along to the radio.

This was what I was protecting. This life, this family, this community.

And I'd do whatever it took to keep it safe.

Chapter Eight

Thursday morning at The Crock Pot started like any other day. I arrived early to prep the soup of the day, tomato basil, and get everything ready for the lunch rush. The familiar rhythm of chopping vegetables and seasoning soup helped settle my mind after yesterday's revelations about Clark Marlowe and the Douglas couple.

I'd started with fresh Roma tomatoes, roasting them until their skins blistered and caramelized. The smell filled the kitchen, sweet and rich. Fresh basil from our herb garden waited on the prep counter, its leaves bright green and fragrant. I'd blend it all together with cream and a touch of honey, finish it with a drizzle of good olive oil. Comfort in a bowl, which was exactly what people needed on a day like this.

By eleven, the restaurant was humming with activity. The lunch crowd had started trickling in, and the sounds of conversation mixed with the clatter of plates and the sizzle of food on the grill. Ava and Skye handled the front of house with practiced efficiency while Marco bussed tables and Smokes worked the dish pit. The comfortable chaos of service always made me feel grounded, connected to something real and immediate.

The ticket machine chattered constantly, spitting out orders. I moved between stations, checking plates, tasting sauces, making sure everything met our standards. The tomato basil soup was selling well, already three refills on the pot and it wasn't even noon yet.

I was plating a chicken and dumplings order, arranging the tender dumplings just so, when Ava appeared at my station. Her ponytail was slightly askew, a sure sign we were getting busy.

"Chef, there's someone here for a pickup order. She's asking to speak with you specifically."

"Did she give a name?" I added a garnish of fresh parsley to the plate and slid it across the pass.

"May Lowen. She said you'd know her."

I felt my stomach tighten. "Tell her I'll be out in a few minutes. Have her wait at the bar."

The bar area sat at the back of the dining room, away from most of the lunch crowd. It was where we usually seated people waiting for takeout orders or anyone who needed to speak privately with management. A row of comfortable stools faced the polished wood counter, and the lighting was softer there, more intimate.

I finished plating the order and handed it off to Marco, then washed my hands at the prep sink. The hot water felt good against my skin, grounding me. I checked my reflection in the stainless steel prep counter, hair still mostly in place, no obvious food stains on my chef's coat. After pulling off my apron and hanging it on its hook, I made my way through the kitchen doors into the dining room.

The lunch crowd was in full swing. Every table seemed to be full, the sound of conversation and laughter creating a warm buzz. I nodded to regulars as I passed, accepting compliments on the soup with a smile. But my attention was focused on the figure sitting alone at the bar.

May sat hunched over the counter, a brown paper bag beside her. She looked even worse than she had yesterday, if that was possible. Her hair was unwashed and pulled back in a messy ponytail, her clothes wrinkled like she'd slept in them. Dark circles shadowed her eyes, and she kept fidgeting with her phone, checking the screen, then setting it down, then picking it up again a moment later.

"May, hi. How are you holding up?"

May looked up with startled eyes, as if she'd been lost in thought. For a moment, she seemed disoriented, like she couldn't quite place where she was. "Oh, Jess. Thanks for seeing me."

"Of course. What brings you by?" I slid onto the barstool next to her, angling myself so I could see her face clearly.

"I ordered some lunch to take back to the farm. The food you brought her on Tuesday really cheered her up, but she hasn't eaten much since." May gestured to the bag with a trembling hand. "She always talks about how good your food is. Says your chicken and dumplings remind her of her grandmother's cooking."

"That's thoughtful of you." I studied her more closely. Her hands weren't just trembling, they were shaking noticeably. And there was a nervous energy about her that set off alarm bells in my head. "How is she today?"

"Not good. She spent the morning on the phone with insurance companies. They're saying the policy might not cover this kind of... deliberate damage." May's voice cracked slightly, and she pressed her lips together like she was fighting tears. "One minute she's talking about rebuilding, the next she's looking into putting the farm up for sale. She keeps going back and forth. It's like she can't decide what she wants anymore."

"Maybe she just needs some time to process everything. It's only been a few days."

"Time is exactly what we don't have." May's response was sharper than necessary, her voice rising slightly. A couple at a nearby table glanced over. May seemed to realize it, and she lowered her voice. "I'm sorry, I didn't mean to snap. It's just... this whole situation is a nightmare."

I reached out and touched her arm gently. "May, you look exhausted. When's the last time you slept?"

"I don't know. Tuesday? Maybe Monday night." She rubbed her eyes with the heels of her hands. "Every time I close my eyes, I see those dead bees. Thousands of them. And I keep thinking about how Honey looked when she first saw them, like her heart was breaking right there in front of me."

There were dark circles under her eyes, and her hands shook slightly as she reached for her coffee cup. I noticed her nails were bitten down to the quick, raw and painful-looking.

"May, can I ask you something? When you and Honey formed your partnership, how did you structure it financially?"

"What do you mean?" She set the coffee cup down with a slight clatter.

"I mean, did you invest money upfront? Do you own part of the business, or are you more of an employee?"

May was quiet for a long moment, staring into her coffee like it might hold answers. Her jaw worked, and I could see her deciding whether to tell me. "I invested my life savings," she said finally, her voice barely above a whisper. "Twenty-five thousand dollars. Honey kept fifty-one percent since it's her family's land, but I own forty-nine percent of the farm operation. The bees, the flowers, the honey production. All of it."

"So, if the farm fails..."

"I lose everything. My investment, my livelihood, my reputation in the agricultural community." May's laugh was bitter, sharp-edged. "Three years of my life, down the drain. Three years of seven-day weeks of working until my hands bled, of pouring every penny I had into making this dream work. And now..."

"But if Honey sells to someone like Clark Marlowe, you'd get half the proceeds, right?"

May's head snapped up, her eyes suddenly sharp and focused. "How do you know about Clark's offers?"

"I met him. He showed up at the farm on Tuesday while I was visiting Honey. Made his pitch right there in the kitchen, the day after the bees died." I couldn't keep the disgust out of my voice. "Real classy guy."

"He has. Every few months, another offer. Always higher than the last one." May was fidgeting with her phone again, turning it over and over in her hands in a compulsive gesture. The screen lit up with each turn, casting a glow across her pale face. "Honey keeps refusing, but..."

"But what?"

"Nothing. Forget I said anything." May stood up abruptly, nearly knocking over her coffee cup. She grabbed her takeout bag, clutching it like a lifeline. "I should get this food back to her while it's still warm."

"May, wait." I stood too, reaching out to touch her arm. She flinched slightly at the contact. "If there's something you know about what happened to the bees, you need to tell the police."

"I don't know anything." May's voice was too high, too fast. The words came out in a rush, tumbling over each other. "I just want this nightmare to be over. I want to wake up and have everything be normal again. Is that too much to ask?"

She headed for the door, moving quickly, her shoulders hunched. Then she paused and looked back, and the expression on her face made my chest tighten. It was guilt, raw and painful.

"Jess, do you think... do you think Honey will ever forgive me?"

"Forgive you for what?"

But May was already walking away, pushing through the door into the bright sunlight outside. I stood there, frozen, my mind racing through possibilities. Forgive her for what? What had May done that required forgiveness?

"Everything okay, Chef?" Ava appeared at my elbow, her order pad in hand. She glanced toward the door where May had just exited. "That lady seemed really upset."

"I'm not sure." I watched through the window as May got into her car, a battered sedan with a dented bumper. She sat there for a moment, her head down, shoulders shaking like she might be crying. "Ava, that woman who was just here. Did she seem... off to you?"

"Definitely. She kept checking her phone like she was expecting a call or something. Every few seconds, she'd pick it up, stare at the screen, then put it down again. And when I brought her the food, she jumped like I'd scared her." Ava lowered her voice. "She looked like my cousin did when he was going through his divorce. That kind of exhausted, desperate look."

"What did she order?"

"Two chicken and dumplings, extra cornbread. But here's the weird thing, she paid with cash. Exact change, like she'd counted it out beforehand. Had it ready in her hand before I even told her the total."

I frowned. Most people paid with cards these days, especially for takeout orders. Exact cash suggested planning, preparation. Or maybe just someone who knew exactly how much money they had left and couldn't afford to go over.

"Thanks, Ava. Can you cover things out here for a few minutes? I need to make a phone call."

"Sure thing, Chef. We've got it under control."

I made my way back through the kitchen, acknowledging a question from Eli about a special order with a quick nod, then slipped into my office. The small room smelled like coffee and the lavender sachets Vee had given me. I sank into my desk chair and pulled out my phone.

May's words kept echoing in my mind. *Do you think Honey will ever forgive me?*

Not "will things work out" or "will we get through this." Will she *forgive* me. That implied guilt, responsibility. That implied May had done something that required forgiveness.

I scrolled to Kyle's number and typed out a message.

Me: May Lowen just came by the restaurant. Acting very strange. Asked if Honey would ever forgive her, then left before I could ask what she meant.

I stared at the message for a moment, then added:

Me: She looked like she hadn't slept in days. Hands shaking. Paid with exact cash. Something's not right.

The response came back quickly, making my phone buzz.

Kyle: Interesting. I've been looking into that business partnership you mentioned. Found some things you might want to know. Want to discuss it over dinner tonight?

My heart did a little flip at the casual invitation. Kyle and I were rebuilding, taking things slow, but dinner three nights in a row felt like progress.

Me: Yes. Can you come to the house? I'll cook.

Kyle: Perfect. See you around 5?

Me: See you then.

I set my phone down and stared out the office window at the parking lot. May's car was gone now, but I could still picture her haunted expression, the guilt written across her face.

Forgive her for what? For losing their investment? For not being able to save the bees? For pushing Honey to sell to Clark Marlowe?

Or for something much worse?

A knock on the door pulled me from my thoughts. Noah stuck his head in, his expression apologetic. "Chef? Sorry to interrupt, but we just got a big party of eight walk in, and table five is asking if we can do something special for their anniversary."

"Be right there." I stood, pushing aside my worries about May and Honey. The restaurant needed me now. The investigation would have to wait until tonight, when Kyle came over and we could compare notes.

As the lunch rush picked up again, I tried to focus on orders and service, on plating beautiful dishes and making sure every customer left happy. But part of my mind kept circling back to May's guilty expression and her strange question about forgiveness.

Whatever May was hiding, I had a feeling we were about to find out. And I wasn't sure any of us were going to like the answer.

Chapter Nine

At 3:30, I picked up the twins from school and drove home, my mind still on May's strange visit. The twins chattered about their day, excited about their science project on butterflies.

"We drew new pictures today!" Ivy announced. "Can we show Kyle?"

"He's coming for dinner, so I'm sure he'd love to see them."

"Yay!" Dove clapped. "These ones have caterpillars on them too!"

By the time we got home, Vee was already there, changed out of her postal uniform and sitting at the kitchen table with a mug of tea, scrolling through her phone.

"Hey, girls. How was school?"

"Good! We drew more butterfly pictures!" Ivy announced, dropping her backpack by the door.

"We're going to show Kyle!" Dove added.

"That's wonderful. I'm sure he'll love them."

Shayla came through the front door a few minutes later, looking tired but managing a smile for her sisters.

"How was work?" I asked.

"Quiet. Honey came in for a few hours this afternoon, but she was just going through the motions. A customer came to pick up a custom order of honey cakes, and when Honey brought them out, she almost started crying right there at the counter."

I felt a pang of sympathy. "It's going to take time."

"I know. I just hate seeing her like this." Shayla hugged both twins. "How are my favorite students today?"

"We have new butterfly pictures to show Kyle!" Ivy said.

"Kyle's coming for dinner?"

"He has some information about the bee situation," I said carefully, mindful of little ears. "Nothing exciting, just business stuff."

Kyle arrived at five o'clock carrying a bottle of wine and a bag of groceries.

"What's all this?" I asked, accepting a kiss on the cheek.

"Dessert supplies. I thought the twins might like to make ice cream sundaes after dinner."

"Kyle!" The twins rushed to greet him, nearly knocking him over with their enthusiasm.

"Hey, troublemakers. What's new?"

"We drew new butterfly pictures today!" Dove announced. "Come see!"

"New ones? I can't wait!"

The twins dragged him to the kitchen table where they'd spread out their artwork. Kyle made all the appropriate sounds of amazement as they explained each drawing in detail.

"This one has a caterpillar," Ivy pointed out. "Because butterflies start as caterpillars."

"And this one is a chrysalis," Dove added. "That's like their sleeping bag where they transform."

"These are incredible," Kyle said, and to his credit, he sounded completely genuine. "You two are really talented artists."

While Kyle admired the artwork, I started dinner. I kept it simple: grilled chicken, rice, and steamed broccoli, comfort food that everyone would enjoy.

After a few more minutes of butterfly discussion, the twins ran off to their room to work on more drawings, promising to show Kyle those ones too before he left.

Kyle wandered into the kitchen, leaning against the counter near where I was cooking. He lowered his voice with a sheepish grin.

"I honestly can't tell the difference between today's pictures and the ones they showed me last night at the restaurant. They look exactly the same to me." He shook his head fondly. "But I'd never say that to them. They get so excited about it."

I smiled, feeling a warmth spread through my chest. "That's sweet. They really do love showing you things."

"I love that they want to share stuff with me." His expression softened. "It means a lot, actually."

We shared a quiet moment before I turned back to the stove, my heart full.

Dinner was easy and comfortable. The twins dominated the conversation with more butterfly facts, and Kyle listened attentively to every one, asking questions that made them light up. After dinner, he helped them build ice cream sundaes with all the toppings he'd brought: chocolate sauce, caramel, sprinkles, whipped cream, and of course, extra cherries.

By eight o'clock, the twins were in their room playing with their dollhouse, giving the adults a chance to talk. Kyle, Shayla, Vee, and I gathered around the kitchen table with coffee.

"Before we get into the case stuff," Vee said, pulling her cardigan tighter, "I had something odd happen at work today. Dale Douglas came in to pick up a package."

I set down my coffee cup. "Dale Douglas?"

"Yeah. Big box, couldn't fit in his mailbox." Vee lowered her voice even though the twins were safely out of earshot. "Return address was from Pennsylvania. Some kind of apiary supply company."

"Apiary? That's beekeeping equipment," Kyle said, his interest clearly piqued.

"That's what I thought. When I mentioned it, he got really nervous. Grabbed the box and practically ran out of there." Vee shook her head. "Strange timing, don't you think? Right after what happened to Honey's bees?"

"Very strange," I said, my mind already working through the implications. "Did he say what was in it?"

"Nope. Just mumbled something about old supplies and left in a hurry."

Kyle pulled out his phone and made a note. "I'll add that to my list of things to check out."

"There's something else," I said. "When I talked to Dale at Dreamy Desserts, he seemed to know a lot about bees. More than someone who just watched a documentary would know."

Shayla leaned forward. "What did he say?"

"He mentioned how the queen controls the colony, how workers know their roles instinctively. Called it a 'perfectly organized society.' When I pointed out he seemed knowledgeable, he backtracked fast. Said maybe he'd seen a documentary."

"But you didn't believe him," Kyle observed.

"It felt off. Like he'd said too much and realized it."

"So," Kyle said, his tone becoming more serious. "I did some digging into May and Honey's business partnership."

"What did you find?" I asked.

"It's interesting. May invested twenty-five thousand dollars for a forty-nine percent stake, like she told you. But here's the thing, the partnership agreement gives her the right to force a sale if the business becomes 'financially unviable.'"

"What does that mean exactly?" Shayla asked.

"If they can't meet their financial obligations for three consecutive months, May can petition to dissolve the partnership and force Honey to sell the property. Even though Honey has majority ownership, that clause gives May significant leverage."

I felt a chill. "And with the bees gone..."

"The farm income drops dramatically. They might not be able to make their loan payments or cover operating expenses."

"So, May could potentially force Honey to sell to Clark Marlowe," Vee said quietly.

"It's possible. And if the property sells for what Marlowe's been offering, May would get a significant return on her investment."

"How significant?" I asked.

"Marlowe's last offer was for four hundred thousand. After paying off debts and expenses, May's forty-nine percent would net her close to a hundred and fifty thousand."

Shayla whistled softly. "That's a lot more than her original twenty-five thousand investment."

"Exactly. And here's another interesting detail: May has been struggling financially. She defaulted on her student loans last year and had her car repossessed six months ago. Had to replace it with some old beater just to get around."

That explained the battered sedan with the dented bumper I'd seen her driving.

"So, she's desperate," I said.

"Desperate enough to destroy those bee colonies?" Kyle asked.

The question hung in the air. Through the thin walls, I could hear the twins playing, their voices a cheerful counterpoint to the serious conversation.

"But how would she get Asian Giant Hornets?" Vee asked. "And know how to handle them safely?"

"That's what I'm still working on. I did find out that May has a degree in agricultural science from Texas A&M. She took several entomology courses."

"So, she'd know about insects," Shayla said.

"More than the average person. And she'd have connections in the agricultural community, people who might know where to get exotic specimens."

I thought about May's behavior at the restaurant, the nervousness, the guilt, the question about whether Honey would forgive her.

"She's hiding something," I said. "The way she acted today, asking if Honey would forgive her... I think she's eaten up with guilt."

"Guilt could mean a lot of things," Kyle pointed out. "Maybe she feels responsible for not protecting the bees better. Or maybe she knows who did it and feels guilty for not speaking up."

"Or maybe she did it herself," Vee said bluntly.

Kyle nodded grimly. "I'm planning to bring her in for questioning tomorrow. See if I can get her to talk."

Just then, my phone buzzed with a text from an unknown number. I glanced at it and felt my blood turn cold.

Unknown: Crime-fighting chef needs to stick to cooking. Don't get involved or else.

I showed the message to the others. Kyle's expression darkened.

"Forward that to me right now. And Jess, I want you to be extra careful. If someone's threatening you, it means you're getting close to something they don't want exposed."

"But close to what?" I asked.

"The truth," Kyle said. "And someone's willing to threaten you to keep it buried."

As if to emphasize his point, my phone buzzed again. This time it was a photo, a picture taken from across the street at the elementary school. My car was clearly visible in the parking lot, and though the angle didn't show the twins themselves, the timestamp confirmed it was from that afternoon during pickup.

The message was clear: they knew my routine, where the twins went to school, and who mattered to me.

Kyle's jaw tightened as he looked at the photo. "That's it. I'm putting a patrol car on your street tonight."

"Kyle, you don't have to—"

"Yes, I do. Whoever this is just threatened not only you but implied a threat to Ivy and Dove." His voice was harder than I'd ever heard it. "I'm not taking any chances."

Vee reached across the table and squeezed my hand. "He's right. This person is escalating."

Shayla had gone pale. "What if they come here? What if they try something when we're home?"

"They won't," Kyle said firmly. "I'll make sure of it. And Jess, I want you to forward both those messages to me immediately. We'll try to trace the number."

I nodded, my fingers shaking slightly as I forwarded the texts. "I should ask Cullen to help too. He can check the security cameras around the elementary school, see if he can find who took that picture."

"That's a good idea," Kyle said.

"And maybe he can dig into Dale's background?" Vee added. "The timing of that package is way too suspicious."

"Do it," Shayla agreed. "Cullen's good at finding things."

I opened my messages and found Cullen's number.

Me: Need your help. Someone's been watching me. Sent a threatening photo taken at the school this afternoon during pickup. Can you check security cameras around Dashwood Elementary? See if you can find who took the picture?

The response came quickly.

Cullen: On it. Give me until tomorrow. I'll come by the restaurant to show you what I find.

Me: Also, can you look into Dale Douglas's background? Vee said he got a package from a Pennsylvania apiary supply company today. And when I talked to him at his bakery, he seemed to know a lot about bees.

Cullen: Interesting. I'll dig into that too.

I set my phone down and looked around the table at my makeshift family. Kyle's protective anger, Vee's steady support, Shayla's worried face. Through the thin walls, I could hear the twins playing, their voices a cheerful reminder of what was at stake.

"We're going to figure this out," Kyle said, covering my hand with his. "Whoever did this made a mistake by threatening you. Now we know they're scared, which means we're getting close."

"Close to what, though?" I asked. "May? Clark? The Douglas couple?"

"That's what we need to figure out." Kyle stood. "I'm going to make some calls, get that patrol set up. Jess, I want you to lock all the doors and windows tonight. Don't open the door for anyone you don't know."

After Kyle left to make his calls, I sat at the table with Vee and Shayla, the threatening messages still burning in my mind. Someone out there was watching me, following me, photographing me.

And they wanted me to stop asking questions.

Baxter appeared from nowhere, jumping onto my lap with his usual lack of grace. He settled in immediately, purring and kneading my leg with his paws. A moment later, Lulu hopped onto the table, walking carefully between the coffee cups to press her head against my hand.

"Even the cats know you're stressed," Vee said softly.

I scratched behind Lulu's ears, feeling the tension in my shoulders ease slightly. "They always know."

Shayla reached over to pet Baxter. "What are we going to do?"

"We're going to be careful," I said, drawing strength from the warm weight of Baxter on my lap and Lulu's steady presence. "And we're going to figure out who's behind this before they hurt anyone else."

Which meant I was asking exactly the right questions.

The game had just become much more dangerous.

Chapter Ten

Friday morning, I decided to stop by Honey's Sweet Treats before work. The twins had volunteered to bring cookies for their class's Friday celebration, and I thought buying them from Honey's bakery would be a small way to show support. Every little bit of business helped, especially now.

The morning air was crisp and cool as I drove the familiar streets to the bakery. Honey's shop sat in what used to be an old hardware store, its windows now displaying tempting pastries instead of hammers and nails. The storefront was painted a cheerful yellow with white trim, and normally there would be flower boxes overflowing with blooms.

The bell above the door chimed as I entered, and I was immediately hit with the warm scent of baking bread and cinnamon. Under other circumstances, it would have been welcoming, comforting.

But today, the familiar smells just made the emptiness of the shop more pronounced. Usually, this place would be bustling with customers at this hour, people picking up their morning pastries and coffee. Today, I was the only one here.

Honey stood behind the counter, but she looked like a shadow of her former self. Her hair hung limply around her face instead of being pulled back in her usual neat bun, and dark circles under her eyes spoke of sleepless nights. She wore her usual floral apron, but it looked rumpled, like she'd thrown it on without caring. The vibrant woman who'd talked about her bees with such passion just days ago seemed to have aged years.

"Morning, Honey. How are you holding up?"

Honey managed a weak smile, but it didn't reach her eyes. "Oh, Jess. I'm... surviving, I suppose. What can I get for you?"

"The twins volunteered to bring cookies to school today. I thought I'd grab two dozen of those sugar cookies with the sprinkles they love. Should be enough for their class plus a few extras for the teachers."

"Of course." Honey moved slowly to the display case, her movements lacking their usual efficiency. She moved like someone underwater, every gesture taking effort. "Those are always popular with the kids. I made a fresh batch this morning, figured I should keep the routine going even if..."

She trailed off, leaving the sentence unfinished. *Even if nobody comes to buy them,* I mentally completed.

The display case was still impressively stocked. Honey was a talented baker, and the selection was beautiful with flaky croissants, glistening cinnamon rolls, and perfectly frosted cupcakes. But I could see several items from yesterday still sitting there, their edges slightly dried. Business was suffering.

As Honey boxed up the cookies, carefully placing wax paper between layers, I leaned against the counter. "Have you given any more thought to what you want to do about the farm?"

Honey's hands stilled, a cookie suspended in mid-air. "I've been trying not to think about it, honestly. But the insurance adjuster called yesterday. They're saying the policy doesn't cover deliberate acts of sabotage." Her voice cracked, and she set the cookie down carefully, like she didn't trust her hands anymore. "Three years of building those colonies, and it's all gone. Just... gone. A hundred and fifty thousand bees, Jess. Do you know how long it takes to build up colonies that strong? How much work goes into keeping them healthy and productive?"

"I'm so sorry, Honey. That's not fair."

"No, it's not." She resumed packing the cookies, but I could see her blinking back tears. "May keeps saying we should cut our losses and sell to Clark Marlowe. Get what we can and start over somewhere else." Honey shook her head, and a tear finally escaped, tracking down her cheek. "But this place, this life, it's all I've ever wanted. My grandmother taught me how to keep bees when I was ten years old. She'd take me out to check the hives early in the morning, before the dew dried. She'd show me which flowers the bees loved best, teach me to read the patterns in their behavior. This isn't just a business to me, Jess. It's a legacy."

I felt my throat tighten at the raw emotion in her voice. "Then don't let anyone pressure you into giving it up."

"I've even been in touch with someone about buying new bees, an apiarist two counties over who has colonies to sell. But I'm scared to bring them in until we know who did this. What if they kill the new ones too? I can't go through that again." Her hands trembled as she sealed the cookie box with tape. "I dream about them, you know. The bees. I hear them buzzing, and then the sound cuts off, just stops completely, and I wake up screaming."

Before I could respond, the front door burst open with enough force to make the bell nearly jump off its hook. Clark Marlowe strode in, his face red with anger and his John Deere cap pushed back on his head. His boots were muddy, tracking soil across Honey's clean floor, and he brought with him the smell of diesel fuel and earth—the same smell I remembered from the farm.

"Honey, we need to talk. Now."

Honey took a step back from the counter, her hand going to her throat. "Clark, I told you—"

"You told me you'd think about it. Well, time's up for thinking." Clark's voice was loud enough to carry throughout the small bakery, bouncing off the walls. "I heard about the insurance company. You're not getting a penny from them, are you?"

"That's really none of your business," Honey said quietly, but I could hear the tremor in her voice.

"It is my business when you're being stubborn about an offer that could save your skin." Clark slammed his hand down on the counter, making the glass display case rattle and Honey flinch. "Four hundred thousand dollars, Honey. Cash. More money than this little hobby farm will ever make you. You could pay off all your debts, walk away clean, start over somewhere else."

I felt my temper rising, heat flooding my face. "Excuse me, but I think you need to lower your voice. You're scaring her."

Clark turned his attention to me for the first time since entering, his eyes narrowing. His face was flushed, whether from anger or exertion I couldn't tell. "Well, well. Jessica Vasquez again. Funny how you keep turning up wherever Honey is."

"Hello, Clark. I see your manners haven't improved since we met at the farm."

"This is between me and Honey. Private business."

"Not when you're yelling at her in her own store, it's not." I moved closer to Honey, positioning myself slightly between her and Clark. "I think you should leave."

Clark's face darkened further, his jaw clenching. "Honey, tell your friend to mind her own business."

"Clark, please," Honey said, her voice barely above a whisper. She was gripping the counter edge so hard her knuckles were white. "Can we discuss this later? I have customers—"

"One customer," Clark corrected, gesturing dismissively at me. "And she can wait." He leaned across the counter, getting too close to Honey's face, invading her space in a way that made my protective instincts flare. "You're out of options, Honey. The bees are dead. The insurance won't pay. Your flower business is going to tank without the bees to pollinate them. How are you going to make your loan payments? How are you going to keep this place running? You're barely covering your costs now, and that's with the honey and flower sales. What happens when those dry up?"

"I'll figure something out—"

"With what money?" Clark's voice was getting louder again, taking on a cruel edge. "You think you can just replace a hundred and fifty thousand bees overnight? You think you can rebuild what took you three years to establish? Do you have any idea how much new colonies cost? How long it takes for them to become productive? You're looking at a year, maybe two, before you'd be back to where you were. And that's assuming you don't get hit again."

The way he said "hit again" made my blood run cold. It sounded almost like a threat.

Honey's eyes filled with tears, her composure crumbling. "I don't know, Clark. I just... I don't know."

"Exactly. You don't know because there is no other option." Clark straightened up, his voice taking on a triumphant tone that made me want to slap the smugness off his face. "My offer is good through the weekend. After that, I'm withdrawing it. And when you can't make your payments and the bank comes calling, I'll buy the property at auction for half what I'm offering you now. So really, you're choosing between four hundred thousand now or two hundred thousand later. That's the math, Honey. Simple as that."

"That's enough," I said, stepping closer and putting myself fully between Clark and Honey. "You need to leave. Now."

Clark laughed, but there was no humor in it. The sound was harsh, grating. "Or what? You'll call the police?" He looked around me, keeping his focus on Honey. "Think about it, Honey. Think about what's best for everyone. May understands. She knows this is the smart play."

"What does that mean?" I asked sharply.

Clark ignored me, keeping his focus on Honey like I wasn't even there. "Three days, Honey. That's all you've got. After that, you're on your own." He headed for the door, his heavy boots thudding on the floor. Then he paused and looked back, his expression hard. "Oh, and you might want to tell your friend here to be careful. Small towns can be dangerous places for people who stick their noses where they don't belong."

The door slammed behind him with enough force to make the windows rattle, leaving the bakery in tense silence.

Through the window, I watched him get into his truck, a large Ford F-250 with a lift kit that looked like it cost more than my yearly salary. On the passenger seat, I could see what looked like agricultural magazines or catalogs spread out. One had a bright yellow cover that caught the sunlight as he slammed the door. It said something about advanced farming techniques.

Honey collapsed onto a stool behind the counter, shaking. Her face had gone pale, and she wrapped her arms around herself like she was cold. "I'm sorry you had to see that. He's never been that... aggressive before. Usually, he's almost friendly when he makes his offers. This was different. Desperate."

"Honey, that was basically a threat. Multiple threats, actually. You need to call the police."

"And tell them what? That a neighbor made me an offer to buy my property?" Honey wiped her eyes with a dish towel, the fabric absorbing her tears. "He didn't technically threaten me."

"He threatened me. And he mentioned May understanding that selling is the smart play. What did he mean by that?"

Honey looked uncomfortable, her gaze dropping to the floor. She twisted the dish towel in her hands. "May has been... pushing for us to accept his offer. She says we need to be realistic about our financial situation. That I'm being emotional instead of practical."

"How long has she been pushing?"

"Since the day after the bees died. She keeps saying we need to cut our losses, that this is a sign we should take the money and run." Honey's voice was small. "She's my partner, my friend. I thought she'd want to fight for the farm as much as I do. But sometimes I wonder if she cares more about the money than the dream."

I felt a chill spread through my chest. "Honey, has May been talking to Clark? Outside of you, I mean. Meeting with him privately?"

"I... I don't know. Why?"

"Just curious." I paid for the cookies, my mind racing through possibilities. If May and Clark were coordinating, if they'd been planning this together... "Listen, if Clark comes back and gets aggressive again, you call the police immediately. And call me too. I mean it, Honey. Don't try to handle him alone."

"I will. Thank you, Jess. For standing up to him. I don't know if I could have done that on my own." She managed a stronger smile, though her eyes were still wet. "You're a good friend."

As I left the bakery with my box of cookies, Clark's words echoed in my mind. *Small towns can be dangerous places for people who stick their noses where they don't belong.* Combined with the threatening text from the night before, it felt like a clear warning. Someone wanted me to back off.

But what really bothered me was what Clark had said about May understanding. How did Clark know what May thought about the situation? Had they been talking? Planning? And if so, was May just being pragmatic about their financial situation, or was there something more sinister going on?

I pulled out my phone and called Kyle as I walked to my car, scanning the street for Clark's truck. He'd driven off, but I felt exposed, vulnerable in a way I hadn't before.

"Hey, what's up?"

"I just witnessed Clark Marlowe basically threatening Honey at her bakery. And Kyle, I think May and Clark might be working together."

"What do you mean?"

"Clark said May understands that selling is the smart play. He said it like they'd discussed it, like he knew her position. How would he know what May thinks unless they've been talking?" The words came out in a rush.

Kyle was quiet for a moment. "I'm bringing May in for questioning this afternoon. But Jess, after what happened last night with those texts, I want you to stay away from this investigation."

"I was just buying cookies—"

"And you ended up in the middle of a confrontation with one of our prime suspects. Jess, Clark essentially threatened you to your face. Promise me you'll be careful."

"I promise." I got in my car and locked the doors, checking my mirrors before starting the engine. "But Kyle, there's something else. Clark's offer is only good through the weekend. If he's behind the bee attack, he's created a timeline to force Honey's hand. Push her to the breaking point and then swoop in with his offer."

"Which means if she doesn't sell..."

"He might escalate things. And I don't think Honey would survive another attack like that. Emotionally, I mean. She's barely holding on as it is."

As I drove toward the school to drop off the cookies, I couldn't shake the feeling that time was running out. For Honey, for the investigation, and possibly for anyone who got in Clark Marlowe's way.

After dropping the cookies with the twins' teacher and accepting her enthusiastic thanks, I decided to make a few stops before picking up the twins. I had some time, and I needed to clear my head after the confrontation with Clark. But even as I went through my errands, part of my mind kept circling back to that bakery, to Honey's tears, and to Clark's threatening words.

Something was coming. I could feel it building like a storm on the horizon. And I had a feeling we were running out of time to stop it.

Chapter Eleven

After dropping off the cookies at Dashwood Elementary, I had some time before I needed to meet Cullen at the restaurant later that afternoon. The confrontation with Clark had left me rattled, and I needed some time to process what I'd witnessed. A few errands would help clear my head.

My first stop was Roasted Beans Coffee. The familiar bell chimed as I entered, and Mallory looked up from behind the espresso machine with a warm smile.

"Jess! Perfect timing. I just finished a new roast I think you'll love." Mallory wiped her hands on her apron and came around the counter for a quick hug. "How are you holding up with everything going on?"

"Everything going on?"

"The bee situation with Honey. The whole town's talking about it." Mallory lowered her voice. "I heard it wasn't an accident."

"Word travels fast around here." I accepted the cup of coffee Mallory handed me. "What are people saying?"

"Mostly just speculation. But I'll tell you what's interesting, I've had some unusual customers lately."

"How so?"

Mallory glanced around the coffee shop. There were only a couple of other customers, both absorbed in their laptops. "You know Dale Douglas? From Dreamy Desserts?"

"Yeah, I know him."

"He's been coming in here every morning for the past week. Orders the same thing every time and sits by the window nursing his coffee. Doesn't really talk much, just stares across the street. But it's more than just people-watching. He takes notes in this little notebook, checks his phone, writes things down. Like he's keeping track of something."

I felt a chill. "Tracking what?"

"Hard to say for sure, but his table faces Honey's bakery. Could be people-watching, could be something else." Mallory shrugged. "Just thought it was odd since I'd never seen him in here before this week."

I walked over to the window and looked out. From this angle, I could see directly across the street to Honey's Sweet Treats. The view was perfect, you could see everyone who went in and out, what time Honey arrived, how busy the place was.

"That is odd," I said, returning to the counter. "Thanks for mentioning it, Mallory."

"Of course. If he keeps coming in here acting strange, I'll let you know."

After promising to be careful, I left Roasted Beans and walked across the parking lot to Heroes and Villains Comics. Monte was arranging new merchandise behind the counter when I entered.

"Jess! Perfect timing. I got some new artwork in yesterday, and there's a piece I think you'll love."

"A new artist?"

"New to us, anyway. She does folk art. Really beautiful, mystical kind of stuff." Monte gestured toward the back wall. "I almost set it aside for you."

I followed him to the art display. The piece that caught my eye immediately was a painting of a woman surrounded by bees, flowers, and woodland creatures. The style was reminiscent of medieval illuminated manuscripts, but with a modern twist.

"It's beautiful," I said, studying the intricate details. "What's the artist's name?"

"Local woman, goes by M. Lowen. She brought in three pieces yesterday, said she was looking to make some extra cash."

My blood turned cold. "M. Lowen?"

"Yeah, nice lady. A bit quiet, seemed like she might be going through a tough time financially." Monte pulled out a small card. "Left her contact info in case I sell anything."

The card read "May Lowen, Agricultural Art, Specializing in Farm and Garden Themes."

"Monte, did she say anything else when she brought them in?"

"Just that she was hoping to supplement her income a bit. Times are tough for a lot of artists." Monte looked at the paintings. "The work is really good quality though."

"Yeah, I know her." I studied the paintings more closely. May was trying to make extra money, which made sense given what Kyle had said about her financial struggles.

"The paintings are reasonably priced," Monte added. "Good value for the quality."

"Monte, if she comes back, will you call me?" I pulled out my phone. "This might be important."

After leaving the comic shop, I realized I needed to pick up a few groceries. I had even more to think about now. May selling her artwork, Dale watching Honey's bakery from the coffee shop. The pieces were starting to connect, but I wasn't sure how yet.

I grabbed a cart and made my way through the produce section, picking up ingredients for the weekend. The twins had requested spaghetti and meatballs again, and I needed fresh basil for the sauce. As I headed toward the checkout lanes, I stopped short.

There, behind register three, wearing a bright green grocery store vest, was Abby Douglas.

I hesitated, considering whether to go to a different lane, but Abby had already spotted me and was waving me over with a forced smile.

"Jessica! What a nice surprise. I'll take you right here."

I pushed my cart to Abby's lane, noting the tight lines around the woman's eyes and the way her usually perfect makeup looked hastily applied.

"Hi, Abby. I didn't know you worked here."

"Oh, this?" Abby gestured to her vest with a laugh that sounded brittle. "Just part-time. You know how it is, keeping busy." She began scanning my items with practiced efficiency. "Dale and I still own and run Dreamy Desserts, of course. This is just a little side thing."

As she reached for a paper bag, I noticed angry red scratches running up her forearms. Fresh ones, not the faded kind you'd get from casual gardening. She caught me looking and quickly pulled down her sleeves.

"Gardening," she said with a brittle laugh that didn't match her eyes. "Rose bushes are vicious this time of year."

"Of course." I watched Abby's hands shake slightly as she scanned a box of pasta. "How's the bakery business?"

"Wonderful! Better than ever, actually." Abby's voice pitched higher. "We've been so busy, especially with all the... recent developments in the area."

The comment felt loaded. "Recent developments?"

"Well, you know." Abby lowered her voice conspiratorially. "Poor Honey's situation. Terrible what happened to those bees. Just terrible."

"It really is."

"Though I have to say, it's opened up opportunities for other local bakers. Customers are looking for alternatives now." Abby's smile was sharp. "Silver lining, I suppose."

I felt my temper rising. "I'm sure Honey would be thrilled to know her tragedy is benefiting your business."

Abby's face flushed. "That's not what I meant. I just meant that when one business struggles, others naturally see an increase. It's basic economics."

"Right. Economics." I handed over my credit card. "And how long have you been working here? At the grocery store?"

"Not long. Just a few weeks." Abby swiped the card with more force than necessary. "Like I said, it's just to keep busy. Dale handles most of the day-to-day operations at the bakery now."

"That's convenient. Gives you both time to pursue other interests."

Something flickered in Abby's eyes. "What do you mean by that?"

"Nothing specific. Just that it's nice when couples can divide responsibilities." I accepted my receipt. "Have you heard anything about who might have been responsible for what happened to Honey's bees?"

"How would I know anything about that?" Abby's voice was too sharp, too defensive.

"I just thought, with you being in the baking community, you might have heard rumors. People talk."

"Well, I haven't heard anything." Abby was already looking past me to the next customer. "I need to keep this line moving."

"Of course. Thanks for checking me out." I paused. "Oh, and Abby? I hope things pick up for you soon. Both at the bakery and here."

I could feel Abby's eyes burning into my back as I walked away.

In the parking lot, I loaded my groceries and checked my phone. Two missed calls from Kyle. I called him back as I got in my car.

"Hey, sorry I missed your calls. I was grocery shopping."

"No problem. I wanted to update you on the May situation."

"What happened?"

"I brought her in for questioning this afternoon. Asked her about her relationship with Clark Marlowe, her financial investment in the farm, her knowledge of insects."

"And?"

"She lawyered up after about ten minutes. But those ten minutes were interesting."

I started my car but stayed parked. "How so?"

"She got very defensive when I asked about Clark. Said they'd never spoken privately, but her body language suggested otherwise. And when I asked about her entomology background, she clammed up completely."

"Did you ask about the night the bees were killed?"

"She claims she was home alone, no alibi. But here's the kicker, when I asked if she thought Honey should sell to Clark, she said it would be the 'smart business decision.' Almost exactly the same words Clark used earlier."

"Like they'd discussed it."

"Exactly. Her lawyer showed up and shut down the interview, but I got enough to know she's hiding something."

I told him about my encounters with Dale watching the bakery and Abby working at the grocery store.

"Interesting timing," Kyle said. "She takes a part-time job right around when their bakery would be feeling the pinch from losing customers to Honey's place."

"She made some comment about recent developments opening up opportunities for other bakers. Like she was happy about Honey's situation."

"I'll pay Dreamy Desserts another visit. See how Dale's doing running things solo."

"Kyle, I keep thinking about what Clark said. About May understanding that selling is smart. What if they've been planning this together?"

"It's possible. May forces the sale through the partnership agreement, Clark gets the land he wants, and May gets a big payout instead of watching her investment slowly fail."

"And Honey loses everything."

"We're going to stop them, Jess. But I need you to promise me you'll stay away from all three of these people. Clark's already threatened you once, and after what happened last night..."

"I promise. But Kyle, what if they try something else? What if they target Honey directly?"

"I've got patrol cars doing extra drives past both the farm and the bakery. And I'm hoping to have enough evidence to make an arrest soon."

After we hung up, I sat in the grocery store parking lot, thinking. Three suspects, all with clear motives and opportunity. But which one had actually gone through with destroying those bee colonies?

And more importantly, what would they do next to protect their secret?

I checked the time. Almost 2:00. I needed to get these groceries home before heading to The Crock Pot to meet Cullen. He'd texted earlier that he'd found some interesting information and wanted to show me what he'd dug up before his shift started at three.

As I drove home, I couldn't shake the feeling that time was running out. Clark's weekend deadline was approaching, and if he didn't get the answer he wanted from Honey, I had a feeling things were about to get much worse.

I pulled into my parking spot at the curb and quickly unloaded the groceries, putting away the perishables and leaving the rest on the counter. Vee and Shayla could help me finish unpacking later.

I grabbed my keys and headed back out. Whatever Cullen had uncovered, I had a feeling it was going to change everything.

Chapter Twelve

I arrived at The Crock Pot at 2:45 to meet Cullen. The lunch rush had wound down, and the kitchen was in that quiet lull between services. I headed straight to the back office.

Cullen was already there, laptop open on the desk. Noah was there too, reviewing invoices, but he looked up when I entered.

"Cullen says he's got something important," Noah said. "Mind if I stay?"

"Please," I said, closing the door behind me.

"Good because I was staying whether you liked it or not." Noah grinned.

I shot him a look, then pulled up a chair next to Cullen. "What did you find?"

Cullen turned his laptop so both of us could see the screen. "I pulled footage from three different cameras around the school. Traffic cameras, the school's security system, and a camera from the gas station across the street."

"And?"

"I couldn't find anyone clearly taking a photo. But look at this." He clicked through several images, zooming in on different angles of the school parking lot. "This is from 3:32 yesterday afternoon. Right around when you would have been picking up the twins."

I leaned closer. In the corner of the frame, partially obscured by a tree, was a shadowy figure. They appeared to be standing near a dark vehicle, and their posture suggested they were holding something up, possibly a phone or camera.

"Can you get a clearer image?" I asked.

"I tried different cameras and angles, but this is the best I could do." Cullen showed me two more images from slightly different perspectives. The figure remained frustratingly indistinct, just a dark shape that could have been almost anyone. "The tree blocks most of the good angles, and they were smart about positioning themselves."

"So, they knew where the cameras were," Noah observed.

"Looks like it. Which suggests this was planned, not spontaneous." Cullen pulled up another window. "I also found this.

Same figure, different day. This was taken Tuesday afternoon, same time, same general location."

I felt a chill. "They've been watching me for at least two days."

"Maybe longer. I'm still going through older footage, but it takes time."

Noah's expression grew darker. "So someone's been stalking you. And threatening you because you're asking questions about Honey's bees."

"That's the theory," I said.

"Which means whoever did it is getting nervous." Noah studied the shadowy figure on the screen. "Can you tell anything about them? Height, build, anything?"

"Hard to say with the angle and the shadows." Cullen zoomed in as far as the image quality would allow. "I'd estimate average height, maybe five-eight to six feet. The build is unclear because of the loose clothing, but I don't think they're particularly large or small."

"So basically anyone," I said.

"Pretty much. Though I can tell you what kind of vehicle they were near." Cullen pulled up another image. "Dark pickup truck, looks like a Chevy or GMC, probably 2015 to 2020 model year based on the body style."

My breath caught. "A dark pickup? I thought someone was following me in a dark pickup on Wednesday. But when I turned down a side street, they kept going straight."

"Or they realized you'd noticed them and backed off," Noah pointed out.

"Can you send all of this to Officer Rafferty?" I asked Cullen.

"Already did. Sent it to him before I headed over here. He's going to have the department's tech analyst take a look, see if they can clean up the image any better than I could." Cullen closed that window and opened another. "Now, about Dale Douglas."

I sat up straighter. "What did you find?"

"Quite a bit, actually. Dale Douglas grew up in Lancaster County, Pennsylvania. His family has been in the beekeeping business for three generations. Douglas Family Apiaries was a well-known operation, supplying honey to local markets and teaching beekeeping classes."

"So, he definitely knows about bees," Noah said.

"More than that. He was actively involved in the business until about four years ago." Cullen pulled up several old social media posts and newspaper articles. "Here's an article from a local Pennsylvania paper about the family business. Dale is mentioned specifically as taking over day-to-day operations after his father semi-retired."

I scanned the article. There was even a photo of a younger Dale standing next to several beehives, wearing a full beekeeping suit and holding up a frame thick with honeycomb.

"What happened four years ago?" Noah asked.

"That's where it gets interesting. I found posts on some beekeeping forums where Dale was asking for advice about varroa mite infestations. Apparently, his colonies got hit hard. From what I can piece together from various posts, he lost most of his hives over the course of about six months."

"That must have been devastating," I said, thinking of Honey's grief over losing her bees.

"It was. There are a few posts from other beekeepers offering condolences and advice, but Dale stopped posting after that. Then, about three and a half years ago, he and Abby moved to Texas and opened Dreamy Desserts." Cullen pulled up the business registration. "No mention of beekeeping anymore. It's like he walked away from the family business entirely."

"Until now," I said quietly. "Vee said he got a package from a Pennsylvania apiary supply company."

"Which I also looked into." Cullen was clearly proud of his detective work. "The company is called Keystone Apiary Supply. They specialize in beekeeping equipment and, interestingly, pest management supplies for beekeepers."

"Pest management?" Noah leaned forward. "Like what kind of pests?"

"Varroa mites, wax moths, small hive beetles, and methods for dealing with hornet infestations." Cullen met my eyes. "Including Asian Giant Hornets."

The three of us sat in silence for a moment, the implications hanging heavy in the air.

"So, Dale has the knowledge," I said slowly. "He has experience with bees, with bee diseases and pests. He just ordered supplies from a company that deals with hornets. And his bakery is failing."

"Means, motive, and opportunity," Noah said. "The classic trifecta."

"But is it enough?" I asked. "Knowing about bees and ordering supplies doesn't prove he destroyed Honey's colonies."

"No," Cullen agreed. "But it makes him a very strong suspect. Especially combined with the fact that someone is following you and threatening you to back off."

"Does Dale drive a dark pickup truck?" Noah asked.

Cullen grinned. "I was hoping you'd ask that." He pulled up the DMV records. "Registered to Dale Douglas: 2017 Chevrolet Silverado. Color: black."

I felt my stomach drop. "It was him. He was following me."

"Maybe," Cullen cautioned. "Or maybe it's a coincidence. Dark pickup trucks are pretty common, especially in Texas."

"I don't believe in coincidences," Noah said firmly. "Not this many, all pointing in the same direction."

I pulled out my phone. "I need to call Kyle. He needs to know about this."

"He'll want to hear your thoughts on it," Cullen said.

Kyle picked up on the second ring. "Hey, Jess. I got Cullen's files. Pretty damning stuff about Douglas."

"That's what we thought. The family beekeeping business, the truck, the package from the pest management company..."

"Yeah. I'm heading out to talk to him this afternoon. Want to see if he'll explain any of this voluntarily before we push harder."

"Be careful. If it is him, he's already shown he's willing to threaten people."

"Always am. I'll call you later, okay?"

"Okay. Stay safe."

I hung up and looked at Cullen and Noah. "He's going to talk to Dale this afternoon."

As I glanced at the laptop screen one more time, I saw the shadowy figure by the dark pickup truck. Dale's family history of beekeeping. The package from the hornet pest management company.

The pieces were coming together. But we still didn't have proof.

And until we did, whoever had killed Honey's bees was still out there, watching, waiting, and willing to threaten anyone who got too close to the truth.

I checked my phone. Almost 3:15. "I need to go pick up the twins from school."

"Be careful," Noah said. "If that dark pickup shows up again, call Kyle immediately."

"I will." I stood and grabbed my purse. "Thanks, Cullen. This is really helpful."

"Anytime, Chef. I'll keep digging, see if I can find anything else."

As I drove to Dashwood Elementary, I couldn't help scanning the road behind me for dark pickup trucks. Every vehicle made me nervous, every shadow seemed threatening.

Whoever was behind this had made it personal. They'd threatened me, followed me, watched my routine with the twins. And now we had three solid suspects, each with motive and opportunity.

But which one had actually done it? And more importantly, what would they do next to protect their secret?

I pulled into the school parking lot and positioned my car where I could see anyone approaching. The twins would be out any minute, and I'd make sure they got safely in the car before we headed home.

This investigation was far from over. But one thing was certain, I wasn't backing down. Not when Honey's livelihood was at stake, and not when someone was threatening my family.

Chapter Thirteen

After picking up the twins from school, I drove home with my mind still spinning from everything I'd learned that day. Dale watching Honey's bakery, May selling her artwork, Abby taking a part-time job. All three suspects showing signs of financial stress or suspicious behavior.

"Can we have a snack?" Ivy asked as we came through the front door.

"Of course. Get your homework started and I'll bring you something."

While the twins settled at the kitchen table with their backpacks, I pulled out apple slices and peanut butter. Vee came through the door just as I was setting the snacks down.

"Perfect timing," I said. "How was your day?"

"Busy. Friday always is." Vee grabbed an apple slice. "But I'm glad to be home. How did your day go? You look like you've got something on your mind."

"Actually, I do. Can you help me with something after the twins get settled?"

"Of course. What kind of help?"

"Research. About Asian Giant Hornets. But I think we're going to need Cullen for this."

Vee raised an eyebrow. "That sounds serious. What kind of research?"

"Dr. Fry said whoever did this had to acquire the hornets illegally and know how to handle them safely. I want to know how someone would go about getting them."

An hour later, the twins were engrossed in a movie in the living room, and I was calling Cullen while Vee cleared the table.

"Hey, Chef, what's up?" Cullen's voice came through the speaker.

"Cullen, I need your computer expertise. Can you help us trace how someone might illegally acquire Asian Giant Hornets?"

"The murder hornets? From the bee farm case?" There was the sound of typing in the background. "Yeah, I can dig into that. What specifically are you looking for?"

"Kyle said someone had to get them through illegal channels. I want to know who's selling them, how they ship them, if there are any local connections."

"Ah, so we're looking at black market exotic animal dealers. Got it. Are you thinking online forums, dark web, or just regular internet with coded language?"

I looked at Vee, impressed as always by Cullen's immediate grasp of the situation. "All of the above?"

"Cool. Give me about an hour and I'll have something for you. I'm heading to the restaurant soon for the evening shift, but I can work on this and send you what I find."

"That would be perfect. Thanks, Cullen."

"No problem, Chef. I'll text you when I have something."

While we waited for Cullen's research, I filled Vee in on everything I'd learned that day. Clark's confrontation with Honey, Dale's suspicious behavior at the coffee shop, May's artwork at the comic shop.

"So, all three suspects are acting strange," Vee summarized. "But which one had the knowledge and connections to pull off something this elaborate?"

"That's what I'm hoping Cullen can help us figure out."

Two hours later, while I was helping the twins with their homework and Vee was starting dinner, my phone buzzed with a text from Cullen.

Cullen: Found some seriously disturbing stuff. Sending you a file. Check your email.

I grabbed my laptop and opened Cullen's email. Attached was a detailed document with screenshots and analysis.

"Vee, come look at this," I called.

We huddled around the laptop while I read through Cullen's findings.

"This is incredible," Vee said, reading over my shoulder. "He found forum posts from someone asking about illegal hornet imports."

The document showed a user called 'AgriScience_23' who had been posting about Asian Giant Hornets for months. They'd asked about shipping live insects, discussed bee colony vulnerabilities, and even mentioned visiting agricultural extension offices in North Carolina.

My phone rang. Cullen.

"Did you get the file?" he asked.

"Just reading through it now. This is amazing work, Cullen."

"Thanks. I'm between the dinner rushes right now, so I have a few minutes. The really disturbing part is the private message threads I found. AgriScience_23 was negotiating with an illegal dealer called 'ExoticDealer_99.'"

"For the hornets?"

"Definitely. They used coded language, but it's clear they were arranging purchase and delivery of 'V. mandarinia,' that's the scientific name for Asian Giant Hornets. The timeline matches perfectly. Final message was four days before Honey's bees were killed."

I felt my pulse quicken. "Can you trace who these users really are?"

"Not directly, but I did location analysis based on their posts. AgriScience_23 mentions Texas A&M agricultural programs, local weather patterns, even a bee conference in Dallas last month."

"That could be any of our suspects," Vee said.

"There's more," Cullen continued. "I found another username in the same transaction, 'BeeHandler_23.' They were discussing delivery logistics and payment methods."

"Two people working together?"

"Looks like it. One doing research, one handling the practical arrangements. Or it could be the same person using multiple accounts to cover their tracks."

I could hear restaurant sounds in the background, plates clinking, orders being called out.

"Cullen, I need to get this to Kyle tonight. Can you send me everything in a format I can show him?"

"Already done. Everything's in that document, organized with timestamps and evidence. But Jess, be careful. This level of planning and the use of deadly insects... this isn't just agricultural sabotage."

"What do you mean?"

"Those hornets can kill humans too. Multiple stings can cause organ failure. If Honey had been checking her hives when they were released..."

The implication hung heavy in the air.

"I have to get back to the kitchen," Cullen said. "But call me if you need anything else. This case just got a lot more serious."

I called Kyle, putting the phone on speaker so Vee could hear.

"Hey, what's up?" Kyle answered.

"Kyle, Cullen found something about the Asian Giant Hornets. Evidence that someone was planning this attack for months. We have forum posts, illegal suppliers, shipping arrangements, the whole thing."

Kyle was quiet for a moment. "Are you serious?"

"Dead serious. Cullen traced online communications between local users and illegal insect dealers. This wasn't random, it was a carefully planned operation."

"I'm still at the station. How soon can you get here?"

I was already saving files to a flash drive. "As soon as Shayla gets home to watch the twins. Maybe thirty minutes?"

"I'll be waiting. And Jess? If you're right about this, it changes everything. This level of premeditation... we're not just talking about agricultural sabotage anymore."

After Kyle hung up, Vee and I looked at each other.

"What do you think he meant by that?" Vee asked.

"I think he means this could be attempted murder," I said quietly, glancing toward the living room where the twins' movie was still playing. "Those hornets are deadly to humans too. If Honey or May had been stung multiple times while checking the hives..."

We fell silent, the weight of that realization settling over us.

About fifteen minutes later, Shayla walked through the front door, dropping her bag by the coat rack with a heavy sigh.

"Long day?" I asked.

"Exhausting. Honey came in again, but she just sat in the back office crying most of the time. I tried to keep things running, but customers kept asking about her and the bees." Shayla rubbed her temples. "Is there anything to eat? I'm starving."

"Leftover chicken and dumplings in the fridge," Vee said. "But Shayla, can you watch the twins for a bit? Jess and I need to run something to the police station for Kyle."

Shayla's eyes widened. "Did you find something?"

"Cullen found evidence that whoever killed the bees planned it for months. Bought the hornets illegally, the whole thing." I grabbed my purse and the folder with the printouts. "We need to get this to Kyle tonight."

"Go. I've got the twins." Shayla was already heading to the living room. "Be careful, okay?"

"We will."

As Vee and I headed out to the car, I couldn't shake the feeling that we'd uncovered something much bigger and more dangerous than agricultural sabotage. Someone had been willing to use deadly weapons against innocent creatures, and potentially against Honey herself.

The question was: which of our suspects had the knowledge, connections, and cold calculation to pull off something this elaborate?

Chapter Fourteen

The drive to the police station was quiet. The folder felt heavy in my hands, weighted with more than just paper. This was evidence of premeditation, of someone planning an attack for months.

The Dashwood Police Station was a small, efficient building on the corner of Broadway and Main Street. The fluorescent lights gave everything a harsh, clinical quality that matched my mood. Kyle met us at the front desk, looking tired but alert. Dark circles shadowed his eyes, and I could tell he'd been running on coffee and determination for days.

"Thanks for coming in tonight," he said, leading us down a narrow hallway to a conference room. "Detective Upton is joining us to review this. With the potential escalation to attempted murder, he wants to be involved."

The word "murder" hung in the air between us. I'd been thinking about the bees, the threats. But hearing it stated so baldly made my stomach clench.

The conference room was the same small, windowless space where I'd been questioned more times than I cared to remember. When Earl was killed on opening night, when Shayla was found holding the gun after her mother and stepfather were murdered, and most recently when Garrett Majors was killed with my knife. The uncomfortable chairs, the long table, the fluorescent lights that made everything look slightly sickly, it was all painfully familiar.

But this time was different. A whiteboard on one wall was covered with notes about the case, photos of the crime scenes pinned up with magnets. I could see images of Honey's destroyed hives and close-ups of dead bees. This time, I wasn't here as a suspect or even a witness. I was here to help.

A few minutes later, Detective Upton arrived, carrying a thick folder and looking serious. His salt-and-pepper hair was slightly disheveled, like he'd been running his hands through it in frustration.

"Chef, Vee," he nodded to us. "Officer Rafferty briefed me on what your tech guy found. This is impressive work."

"He's pretty amazing with computers," I said, settling into a chair across from Kyle. The metal was cold through my jeans. "What do you think about the evidence?"

Detective Upton spread out several printed pages on the table. I could see forum screenshots, shipping invoices, chat logs with suspicious content. He arranged them methodically, creating a timeline of communication.

"It changes everything. The level of premeditation, the illegal acquisition, the specialized knowledge required. This isn't agricultural sabotage anymore." He tapped one of the printouts. "Look at this conversation thread. It starts three months ago. Three months of planning, researching, arranging shipments."

"What do you mean?" Vee asked, leaning forward to read the text.

"Asian Giant Hornets can kill humans. Multiple stings cause organ failure, respiratory distress, potentially death. If Honey had been checking her hives when these were released..." Upton's expression was grim. "We could be looking at attempted murder."

I felt a chill spread through my chest. Honey checked her hives every morning. She talked to her bees, she told me once, like they were old friends. If she'd been there when the hornets were released, if she'd gotten stung multiple times while trying to protect her colonies...

"Do you think that was intentional?" My voice came out smaller than I intended.

"Hard to say. But whoever did this knew the risks. They researched these insects extensively, understood their lethality." Kyle pointed to one of Cullen's screenshots. "Look at this forum post where AgriScience_23 asks about 'optimal release timing for maximum impact.' They weren't just trying to kill bees."

I read the text, feeling sick. The user had asked specifically about when bees would be most active, when a beekeeper would be most likely working the hives. When the maximum number of bees would be present to attract the hornets' attention.

"They wanted to ensure the attack would be devastating," Vee said quietly.

"Exactly. And the coordination between AgriScience_23 and BeeHandler_23 suggests either one person using multiple accounts or two people working together." Detective Upton pulled out his notebook, flipping to a marked page. "The communication pattern is interesting. AgriScience_23 asks technical questions, BeeHandler_23 provides agricultural context. It reads like two people with complementary knowledge."

"Or one very smart person covering their tracks," Kyle added.

Upton nodded. "Officer Rafferty has been handling the interviews. Kyle, tell them what you've learned."

Kyle pulled out his own notes, and I noticed his handwriting was getting messier, rushed. He'd been working this case hard. "Based on what you've observed, who has the knowledge and means to pull this off?"

I considered the question carefully, thinking through each suspect's background and capabilities. "May has the agricultural background and entomology training. She studied insect biology in college, worked for the extension office. She'd know exactly what these hornets could do and how to handle them safely. She's also been struggling financially and could benefit from forcing Honey to sell."

"What about Clark Marlowe?"

"He's been pressuring Honey to sell for over a year. He has farming experience, runs a large agricultural operation. But I don't know about his insect knowledge specifically. And he definitely has the money to purchase illegal specimens. If you can buy something, Clark can afford it."

"And the Douglas couple?"

"Abby and Dale are desperate. Their bakery is failing, Abby's working at a grocery store now just to make ends meet. They'd benefit from eliminating competition, especially Honey's bakery which is thriving while theirs is dying." I paused, thinking about what Cullen had uncovered. "And Dale definitely has bee knowledge. His family ran an apiary in Pennsylvania for three generations. He knows exactly how to handle bees, and he'd know how to destroy them too."

Kyle made notes as I spoke, his pen moving quickly across the page. "Here's what I've learned from my interviews. May lawyered up quickly when I pressed about her relationship with Clark. She also used almost identical language to Clark when discussing whether Honey should sell. Phrases like 'time to move on,' 'fresh start,' 'too much emotional attachment to make smart business decisions.'"

"Like they'd been talking," Vee observed.

"That's what I think. And Dale Douglas has been watching Honey's bakery from the coffee shop every morning this week. Just sitting there for hours, watching who comes and goes."

"Mallory mentioned that," I said. "She thought it was odd. Said he looked angry, intense."

"It is odd. Unless he's gathering intelligence. Figuring out Honey's schedule, when she's vulnerable." Kyle flipped through his notes. "I also ran financial checks on all three suspects. May defaulted on student loans last year and had her car repossessed six months ago. She's been living in her business partner's guest house, essentially rent-free, because she can't afford her own place."

"She invested her savings in the partnership," I said, remembering her confession at The Crock Pot.

"Twenty-five thousand dollars, according to the partnership agreement. Which is now tied up in a farm she can't access unless Honey sells." Kyle continued. "The Douglas couple is three months behind on their business loan. The bank is threatening foreclosure. They have about six weeks before they lose everything."

"And Clark?" Vee asked.

"Clark Marlowe, on the other hand, is financially secure. Property holdings worth over three million, no significant debt, excellent credit. He doesn't need Honey's land, but he wants it."

"So, May and the Douglas couple are desperate, but Clark has resources," I summarized, trying to process it all.

"Right. And here's something interesting. I checked with local veterinarians and agricultural supply stores. Someone purchased a specialized protective suit designed for handling dangerous insects about six weeks ago. Not just any beekeeper suit, but the kind used for handling aggressive species. Heavy-duty canvas, reinforced gloves, military-grade mesh on the veil."

"Did you find out who?" I asked, feeling my pulse quicken.

"Paid with cash, no name given. But the description matches someone of average height, possibly female. They claimed it was for research purposes. The clerk at Agricultural Supply remembered because it was an unusual purchase. They normally only stock basic beekeeping gear."

Vee and I exchanged a look. "That could be any of our suspects."

"Unfortunately, yes. May is five-foot-six, Abby is about the same height. And someone could have been buying it for Clark." Kyle gathered the papers into neat stacks. "But combined with Cullen's online evidence, we're getting a clearer picture. I'm planning to execute search warrants tomorrow. Look for the protective equipment, any remaining hornets, evidence of the online communications. Computer records, shipping receipts, anything connecting our suspects to AgriScience_23 or BeeHandler_23."

"All three suspects?"

"I need more specific evidence to target one person. Right now, I have enough for search warrants but not arrest warrants. The threshold for arrest is much higher. I need probable cause, not just reasonable suspicion." Kyle stood, starting to pace. "But there's something else. Clark's weekend deadline is tomorrow. If he doesn't get the answer he wants from Honey..."

"You think he might escalate?"

"I think someone might. The timeline is accelerating. Four days ago, bees died. Yesterday, someone was photographing you at the twins' school and sending threatening texts. Whoever's behind this is watching you, tracking your movements." He didn't finish the thought, but he didn't need to.

"Which is why I need you both to stay away from all three suspects this weekend. No more investigating, no casual encounters, no grocery store runs where you might bump into Abby Douglas." Kyle's voice was firm, his expression serious in a way that made my chest tight.

I felt a flutter of guilt about that encounter at Food King. "Understood."

"I'm serious, Jess. Whoever did this planned for months, used deadly weapons, and is now getting desperate. Clark's deadline, the pressure on Honey, your investigation getting closer to the truth. It's a volatile situation. Desperate people make dangerous decisions."

Detective Upton stood as well. "We'll have patrol cars driving by your house regularly. And Honey's farm. If you see anything suspicious, anything at all, you call 911 immediately. Don't investigate, don't confront, don't try to handle it yourself."

As we prepared to leave, Kyle walked us to the front door. The night air felt cold after the stuffy conference room. "There's one more thing. Riley and Sawyer's baby shower is Sunday afternoon, and I want you to be extra careful. Big gatherings, lots of people coming and going. Perfect opportunity for someone to slip in unnoticed, especially if everyone's distracted by the celebration. Just keep your eyes open, stay in groups, don't wander off alone."

The weight of his concern settled over me like a blanket. "You really think someone might try something at the shower?"

"I think someone who's already sent threats won't hesitate to escalate further. And if they're watching your movements, they'll know about the shower." He reached out and squeezed my hand briefly. "Just be careful, okay?"

In the parking lot, Vee and I sat in the car for a moment, processing everything we'd learned. The interior light cast harsh shadows across her face.

"It's really happening," Vee said. "Kyle thinks he can solve this."

"But not before this weekend. Clark's deadline, the search warrants, the baby shower." I started the car, my hands trembling slightly on the steering wheel. "I have a feeling things are about to get complicated."

"At least we'll all be together at the shower. Safety in numbers."

"Yeah." But I couldn't shake the feeling that bringing everyone together might not be as safe as Vee thought. If one of our suspects was getting desperate, if they knew they were running out of time before the police closed in, a gathering of all the people involved in the investigation might be too tempting a target. We'd be predictable, all in one place, distracted by celebration.

As we drove home through the dark streets of Dashwood, I thought about the forum posts, the careful planning, the months of preparation. Someone had been watching Honey, studying her patterns, waiting for the perfect moment to strike. And now, with their plans falling apart, with police attention intensifying, they might be ready to do something even more drastic.

I made a mental note to talk to Sawyer about security for the baby shower. Maybe Kyle could be there in an official capacity. Maybe we could set up at her house instead of a public venue where it would be harder to control who came and went. Because after everything

Kyle had told us, after seeing those detailed forum posts and understanding the depth of planning involved, I wasn't taking any chances with the people I loved.

The weekend was going to be crucial. One way or another, this case was about to reach its conclusion. I just hoped we'd all be safe when it did.

Chapter Fifteen

Saturday morning arrived with the kind of crisp spring air that promised a beautiful weekend. I was making pancakes for the twins when my phone rang. Kyle's name appeared on the screen.

"Morning," I answered, flipping a pancake. "Everything okay?"

"We executed the search warrants this morning. All three suspects."

I nearly dropped my spatula. "What did you find?"

"That's the thing. Nothing concrete yet. May's place was clean, no protective equipment, no evidence of the online accounts. Same with the Douglas couple."

"What about Clark?"

"Now that's where it gets interesting. We found a protective suit in his barn, but Clark seemed genuinely surprised by it. And here's the thing, it's a size small. Clark's a big guy, probably an extra large."

"So, someone planted it there?"

"That's what it looks like. But Clark's still furious about the search, about the implication that he's involved. He's threatening to sue the department, calling the mayor."

I felt a chill of worry. "How furious?"

"Furious enough that I'm concerned about what he might do next. His weekend deadline for Honey is tomorrow, and now he feels like we're working against him."

"Kyle, you need to keep an eye on him."

"We are. But Jess, be extra careful this weekend. If someone's trying to frame Clark by planting evidence, they're getting desperate."

The pancake on the griddle started to burn. I quickly flipped it, my hands shaking slightly. "What about Dale? Did you find anything at his place?"

"Nothing obvious. But there was something odd. He had fresh dirt tracked all through his house, like he'd been doing outdoor work recently. And when we questioned him and Abby, they were making comments, the kind that make me think you need to be extra careful this weekend."

"What kind of comments exactly?"

"Dale said, and I quote, 'We're just trying to run a business, just like anyone else. I wish people would just mind their business and stay out of ours.'"

A chill ran down my spine. "That sounds like a threat."

"It felt like one. And we found a notebook with what looked like surveillance notes, times and dates, but he claimed they were for bakery deliveries."

"Times and dates?"

"Yeah. I went to talk to Mallory about what you told me. She confirmed he'd been taking notes while watching Honey's bakery. This might be what she saw."

"It all sounds so suspicious."

"It is. But it's not enough for an arrest. Same with Abby, she had scratches all over her arms. Said they were from rose bushes, but they looked fresh. Like she'd been struggling with something."

My mind flashed back to seeing those scratches at the grocery store. I'd thought they looked odd then.

After Kyle hung up, I stared at the phone, processing what I'd learned. Someone had planted evidence to frame Clark. The real perpetrator was still out there, and they were getting desperate enough to try framing someone else.

"Everything okay?" Shayla asked, coming into the kitchen with the twins.

"The police searched our suspects this morning. Clark Marlowe is not happy about it."

"What does that mean for us?"

Before I could answer, my phone buzzed with a text from an unknown number.

Unknown: You should have minded your own business. Now you'll pay the price. Both of you.

My blood ran cold. Both of you. That had to mean me and Honey. I was the one asking questions, and she was the one refusing to sell.

"Shayla, maybe you should take the twins to Granny and Auntie Rita's house today. Just to be safe."

"With the baby shower tomorrow? Let's wait and see what happens. But I'll keep the twins close, and we'll stay inside."

I wanted to argue, but I understood. The baby shower was important to all of them, and running away wouldn't solve anything. Besides, running might scare the twins, and they were finally getting comfortable again after what happened with Zane. Still, the threat hung heavy in my mind. If someone was targeting me and Honey, everyone around us could be in danger too.

My phone rang. This time it was an unknown number.

"Hello?" I answered cautiously.

"Jessica, it's Honey. I just got a terrible phone call."

"What kind of phone call?"

"Someone called the bakery this morning. Said that if I don't accept Clark's offer by tomorrow, something worse than dead bees is going to happen." Honey's voice was shaking. "They said they knew where I lived, where I worked, and that they could get to me anytime."

I felt sick. "Honey, did you call the police?"

"I called Officer Rafferty right after. He said they're increasing patrols around the bakery and the farm."

"Good. Honey, I think you should close the bakery today. Maybe stay with friends or family."

"I can't. I have Riley's baby shower cake to finish. I promised I'd have it ready by tomorrow morning."

"Honey, your safety is more important than a cake."

"But it's my business, Jessica. If I start hiding, if I start giving in to these threats, what's next? Do I just let Clark have everything because someone scared me into it?"

I understood that defiance, that refusal to be bullied. But I also understood how dangerous our situation had become.

"At least don't work alone. Have May come in or ask Kyle to have an officer stay at the bakery while you work."

"May's been acting strange lately. Jumpy, nervous. I don't think she wants to be around the bakery right now."

Another red flag. May, who had been pushing Honey to sell, was now avoiding the bakery when things got dangerous.

"Then definitely ask for police protection while you finish the cake."

After we hung up, I paced the kitchen. Threatening texts to me, a threatening phone call to Honey. Someone was escalating, getting desperate.

Vee came into the kitchen, her expression worried. "I heard you on the phone. What's going on?"

I showed her the threatening text. "Kyle executed search warrants this morning on all three suspects. Someone's not happy about it."

"And now they're threatening you and Honey?" Vee's face paled. "Jess, maybe we should all go stay somewhere else for the weekend."

"That's what I suggested to Shayla, but with the baby shower tomorrow..." I shook my head. "And don't you think it might scare the twins if we leave? I've tried several ways in my head how I would explain it to them, but they're smart, they'll see through it."

Vee nodded slowly. "They are smart, and you might be right. We'll just keep them close and watch our security cameras today for anything weird."

"Kyle said to stay together and keep our phones close. He's increasing patrols too."

"Good. Because I'm not leaving you alone today."

While I waited, I called Sawyer to warn him about the threats and the potential danger at tomorrow's baby shower.

"Maybe we should postpone," Sawyer said after I explained everything.

"That's up to you and Riley. But Kyle thinks this will all come to a head soon. The search warrants, Clark's deadline tomorrow, the increasing threats. Someone's going to make a move."

"Then maybe it's better to get it over with. Have everyone together where we can watch out for each other."

"That's what I was thinking too. Safety in numbers."

"Plus," Sawyer added, "Riley's been looking forward to this for weeks. She'll be devastated if we cancel."

I stared at the phone long after we'd hung up, waiting for the next threat, the next escalation. Clark's deadline was tomorrow. The baby shower was tomorrow. And someone out there was angry enough to threaten multiple people.

Whatever was going to happen, it was going to happen soon.

I just hoped we could figure out who was behind it before someone got hurt.

As if summoned by my thoughts, my phone buzzed with another text.

Unknown: Enjoy your last quiet evening.

This time, I didn't hesitate. I forwarded the message to Kyle and called him immediately.

"That's the fourth threat in two days," Kyle said after I read it to him. "We're dealing with someone who's completely lost control."

"What do we do?"

"We catch them. Tomorrow, one way or another, this ends."

Chapter Sixteen

Sunday morning arrived bright and clear. But today was Riley and Sawyer's baby shower, and despite the anxiety that had kept me tossing and turning most of the night, I had a party to throw.

The house was already bustling with activity when I came downstairs. Shayla was at the kitchen table with the twins, who were both bouncing with excitement.

"We're helping with decorations!" Ivy announced.

"Sawyer said we could blow up balloons!" Dove added.

"That's right," I said, smoothing a hand over each of their heads. "After breakfast, we've got a lot to do."

Vee emerged from her room looking tired but determined. "Coffee first, then world domination."

"The shower isn't until one," I said, pouring coffee for both of us. "But we need to start decorating by nine if we want everything perfect."

Kyle had texted earlier that morning, reminding me to be careful and that he'd have patrol cars doing extra sweeps through the neighborhood. The thought should have been comforting, but it just reminded me how serious our situation had become.

By eight-thirty, we'd all eaten breakfast and were ready to transform the house. Riley and Sawyer would arrive around noon to help with final touches, and guests would start arriving at one.

"Okay, team," I announced, surveying my crew. "Shayla, you're on food prep with me. Vee, you're in charge of decorations with the twins. Kyle's coming by around ten to help with the heavier stuff."

"What heavier stuff?" Vee asked.

"Tables, chairs. We're setting up on the patio since the weather's so nice. Plus, Sawyer's dad is bringing something."

"What's he bringing?" Shayla asked.

"I don't know. Sawyer said it was a surprise."

The twins immediately launched into their balloon-blowing duties, with Vee supervising and tying them off. Soon, the living room was filled with cheerful pastel colors, soft yellows, mint greens, and gentle pinks.

"We don't know if it's a boy or girl, right?" Ivy asked.

"Actually, it's a girl," Vee said with a smile. "So, we're doing lots of pretty colors."

"A baby girl!" Dove clapped her hands. "Can we make extra pink balloons?"

"Absolutely. Pink it is."

In the kitchen, Shayla and I worked side by side, falling into the easy rhythm we'd developed over months of cooking together. I had planned a menu of crowd-pleasers: chicken salad tea sandwiches, deviled eggs, fruit salad, vegetable crudités with ranch dip, mini quiches, and pasta salad.

"These sandwiches are so pretty," Shayla said, carefully arranging cucumber sandwiches on a platter. "Riley's going to love everything."

"I hope so. She and Sawyer deserve a perfect day." I piped filling into deviled eggs, my hands steady despite my nerves. "How are you doing? With everything that's been going on?"

"Scared," Shayla admitted quietly. "But trying not to show it around the twins. They're so excited about the party."

"We'll get through this. Kyle's close to figuring it out."

At ten o'clock sharp, Kyle arrived carrying folding tables. Behind him was Sawyer's dad, Roy Hart, a weathered man in his late fifties with kind eyes and calloused hands. He was carrying what looked like a large wooden board.

"Morning, ladies," Roy said, his voice gravelly but warm. "Where do you want this?"

"What is it?" I asked.

Roy grinned. "Sawyer asked me to make something special for the baby. Figured I'd bring it by early."

He turned the board around, and I felt tears prick my eyes. It was a beautiful wooden sign, carefully carved and stained, that read: "Welcome Baby Hart" with space below for the baby's name and birthdate to be added later. Around the edges, Roy had carved delicate images of baby items, rattles, bottles, tiny footprints.

"Roy, this is beautiful," Vee breathed.

"Ah, it's nothing. Just a little something." But he was clearly pleased by our reaction. "Thought they could hang it in the nursery."

"They're going to love it," Kyle said, helping Roy carry it inside.

The twins immediately crowded around, oohing and aahing over the carvings. Roy showed them how he'd made each detail, his patience with them reminding me why Sawyer had turned out so well despite his parents being gone so much during his childhood.

"Mr. Hart, can you teach me to carve?" Dove asked.

"When you're a bit older, sure thing. But for now, how about you two help me set up these tables on the patio?"

By eleven o'clock, the small patio area behind the townhouse had been transformed. The space wasn't much, maybe fourteen by twenty feet, but we'd managed to fit two tables covered with cheerful tablecloths and arranged chairs around them. Vee and the twins had strung up balloon garlands along the back fence and hung paper lanterns from the patio cover. In the center of each table sat small mason jars filled with fresh flowers from Honey's farm. The rest of the seating would have to be inside, but the open floor plan meant people could flow easily between the kitchen, living room, and patio through the door by the twins' room.

I was arranging the last of the food on the buffet table when my phone buzzed. An unknown number.

My stomach dropped.

Unknown: Enjoy the party. Hope nothing ruins it.

I showed it to Kyle immediately.

"That's the fifth threat," he said grimly. "I'm calling it in. We're going to have officers here all afternoon."

"Kyle, I don't want to scare the guests."

"Would you rather risk something happening?" His tone was sharp, but then he wrapped an arm around me and pulled me close. "Sorry. I'm just worried. Whoever this is, they're escalating. They know about the party, which means they've been watching."

Before I could respond, a white van pulled up to the curb. Honey climbed out, carefully extracting the most beautiful cake I had ever seen from the passenger seat.

It was a Russian honey cake, layers upon layers of thin golden cake with billowy whipped frosting between each one. The exterior was covered in smooth frosting and decorated with delicate piped flowers made from honey-infused buttercream. On top, Honey had created a fondant stork carrying a pink bundle, and around the base, she'd piped "Welcome Baby Hart" in elegant script.

"Oh my gosh," Shayla breathed, coming out to see. "Honey, it's gorgeous."

Honey managed a tired smile. "I'm glad you like it. I wanted to do something special for Riley and Sawyer. This is my babushka's recipe, passed down through generations. Each layer is made with honey from my hives." Her voice caught. "Or at least, it was."

As we carefully carried the cake to the kitchen, I noticed how exhausted Honey looked, dark circles under her eyes and her hands trembling slightly.

"Are you okay?" I asked quietly.

"Just tired. May came by yesterday afternoon to help me finish the cake, despite everything. I think she needed to feel useful, even though she's been so jumpy lately." Honey set the cake down gently on the counter. "She's back at the farm today, checking on things. I can't stay long either. I need to get back and make sure everything's alright."

At twelve-thirty, Riley and Sawyer arrived. Riley was glowing, her baby bump prominent under a flowing floral dress. Sawyer couldn't stop smiling, his hand protectively on Riley's back as they walked up the front path.

"You guys!" Riley's eyes filled with tears when she saw the decorations. "This is beautiful!"

"Wait until you see what my dad made," Sawyer said, leading her inside.

When Riley saw Roy's carved sign, she burst into happy tears. "Roy, this is perfect. Thank you so much."

Roy shuffled his feet, embarrassed but pleased. "Glad you like it. Figured the little one needs something special."

Sawyer's mom, Linda, arrived moments later. She was a petite woman with warm eyes and graying brown hair pulled back in a practical ponytail. She worked as a nurse at Dashwood General and had taken a rare day off for the shower.

"Jessica, Genevieve, Shayla," Linda greeted each of us with hugs. "Thank you so much for organizing this. You have no idea how much it means to us."

Riley's parents arrived next, her father, Victor, a tall man with Riley's same expressive eyes, and her mother, Diana, who immediately started fussing over her daughter.

"Are you feeling alright? Do you need to sit? Should I get you water?" Diana asked.

"Mom, I'm fine," Riley laughed. "Stop worrying."

"I'm your mother. It's my job to worry."

By one o'clock, the house was full. Granny Ines and Auntie Rita arrived together, both carrying beautifully wrapped gifts. They'd known Sawyer since he was twelve, when he'd first become friends with me, and they treated him like family.

"Mijo," Granny Ines hugged Sawyer tightly. "A baby! I'm so happy for you."

"Thanks, Granny Ines. That means a lot."

Monte and Mallory came together, followed by Noah with his girlfriend April. Colby, a firefighter friend of Riley's, showed up with a massive gift basket. Even Detective Upton and Officer Perez stopped by briefly to drop off gifts and congratulate the parents-to-be.

I was surprised when Max Reeder walked through the door, followed moments later by Elias Cortez. Both had gone to school with us, and both had briefly dated Vee.

"Max! Elias!" Vee's face lit up, though I noticed a slight flush to her cheeks. "I didn't know you were coming."

"Sawyer invited me," Max said, giving Vee a friendly hug. "Said it was a big deal."

"Riley invited me," Elias added, also hugging Vee. "Couldn't miss celebrating their baby girl."

The two men noticed each other and exchanged slightly awkward nods. I had to hide my smile. Vee's dating history with both of them had been brief but memorable.

"Well, the food's on the island," Vee said, gesturing toward the kitchen. "Help yourselves."

As Max and Elias headed toward the food, I caught Vee's arm and pulled her aside into the corner of the kitchen.

"You never told me what happened with these guys," I said quietly, watching Max and Elias navigate around each other at the buffet table.

Vee shrugged, but I noticed the way her eyes kept drifting back to them. "Meh, it just didn't work out."

"That's all I get? 'It didn't work out?'"

"What else is there to say?" She picked up a napkin and started folding it, not meeting my eyes. "Max was great, Elias was great. Neither of them were right, I guess."

"But you're blushing."

"I am not." She touched her cheeks, which only made her blush more. "Okay, maybe a little. It's just awkward having them both here."

"I noticed they noticed each other."

"Yeah, well." Vee finally looked at me, a rueful smile on her face. "I should probably stop trying to date guys from high school. It never works out."

"Or maybe the right one just hasn't happened yet."

"Maybe." She glanced over at the guys again. Max was laughing at something Sawyer said, and Elias was helping Riley reach a plate on the buffet. "Anyway, I should go make sure the punch bowl stays full."

She squeezed my hand and slipped away, but I noticed throughout the rest of the party how her gaze kept finding Max and Elias. When Max carried a chair out to the patio, Vee watched. When Elias knelt down to talk to the twins, showing them something on his phone, Vee's expression softened. She wasn't over either of them, that much was clear. But she was trying to move on.

The house and small patio filled with laughter and conversation. The twins ran around playing with other children who'd come, their excitement about the party infectious.

I was refilling the punch bowl when Vee sidled up next to me.

"This is nice," Vee said, looking around at all our friends and family gathered together. "Riley and Sawyer deserve this."

"They really do," I agreed, though I couldn't shake the uneasy feeling that had settled in my stomach since the threatening text.

Before we could say more, Riley called for everyone's attention from the living room.

"Thank you all so much for being here today," Riley said, her voice thick with emotion. "Sawyer and I are so grateful to have such amazing friends and family. This baby girl is already so loved."

Sawyer wrapped his arm around her. "We couldn't do this without all of you. Especially Jess, Vee, and Shayla for putting this all together. And my parents for..." He got choked up. "For everything. Always."

Roy wiped his eyes. Linda was already crying.

As everyone applauded, I felt my phone buzz again. Another text from an unknown number.

Unknown: Time's up. You should have stayed out of it.

I showed Kyle, who immediately pulled out his phone.

"I'm calling for backup," he muttered. "This isn't just threats anymore. This is—"

He was cut off by a scream from the front of the house.

Everyone froze.

Kyle and I ran toward the sound, with Sawyer right behind us. We found Honey standing on the front porch, staring at her car. All four tires had been slashed. On the windshield, written in what looked like red paint, were the words: "SHOULD HAVE SOLD."

"Oh my God," Honey whispered. "They were here. While we were all here, they were right outside."

Kyle immediately got on his radio. "This is Officer Rafferty. I need units at 1404 Willow Lane immediately. We have vandalism and credible threats. Possible suspect still in the area."

Guests were starting to crowd onto the porch. Roy pulled the twins back inside, shielding them from the sight. Linda herded other children away from the windows.

"Everyone inside," Kyle ordered. "Nobody leaves until we've secured the area."

Victor and Colby helped move everyone back into the house. I noticed Honey standing frozen by her vandalized car, tears streaming down her face.

"Honey," I said gently, guiding her inside. "Come on. Let's get you inside."

Kyle was on his radio, coordinating with dispatch. Through the window, I could see patrol cars pulling up. Officers fanned out to search the neighborhood.

And somewhere out there, someone who'd killed thousands of bees, threatened multiple people, and had just committed vandalism in broad daylight during a baby shower with dozens of witnesses.

"This is escalating," Kyle said quietly to me once Honey was settled on the couch with Riley's mother. "Whoever did this is getting desperate. And desperate people do dangerous things."

I looked around at all the people I loved, gathered in my home for what should have been a joyful celebration. The twins were huddled with Roy and Linda, looking scared. Sawyer had his arm around Riley, protective and tense. Granny Ines and Auntie Rita sat close together, worry etched on their faces.

The baby shower had just turned into a crime scene.

And somewhere out there, the person responsible was still free.

Chapter Seventeen

The living room felt crowded with everyone pressed inside, away from the vandalized car out front. Riley sat on the couch with Sawyer's arm around her, one hand protectively on her baby bump. The twins huddled close to Roy and Linda, their earlier excitement about the party completely forgotten.

I stood by the window, watching Kyle coordinate with the other officers who'd arrived. Two patrol cars now blocked the street, and uniformed officers were taking photos of Honey's car and canvassing the immediate area.

Detective Upton's unmarked sedan pulled up five minutes later, followed closely by Officer Tommy Roberts in another patrol car. I felt a mixture of relief and dread. Upton would take this seriously, but his presence also meant things had officially escalated beyond simple threats.

Through the window, I watched Kyle brief both of them, gesturing toward the house and then back to Honey's car. Upton's face was grim as he listened, nodding occasionally. Officer Roberts pulled out his notepad and started taking notes.

"Jess," Vee touched my arm gently. "You should sit down. You look pale."

"I can't. I need to see what's happening."

"They're professionals. They'll figure this out."

"But what if they don't? What if whoever did this comes back?" My voice dropped to a whisper. "Vee, the twins are here. Shayla. All our friends. What if something had happened during the party?"

Vee squeezed my hand. "But it didn't. Everyone's safe."

A knock on the door made several people jump. Kyle opened it and stepped aside to let Detective Upton and Officer Tommy Roberts enter.

"Everyone okay in here?" Upton's eyes swept the room, taking in the crowd of party guests who'd become witnesses.

"We're fine," I said. "Just shaken up."

"I can imagine. Honey, I'm so sorry about your vehicle." Upton's familiar tone reflected years of knowing the local business owner. He turned to address the room. "I know this isn't how anyone expected this celebration to go, but I need to ask everyone to stay put for a bit while we gather information. Officer Roberts and Officer Rafferty will be taking statements from anyone who might have seen or heard something."

"How long will this take?" Victor asked. "My wife and I need to get Riley home. This stress isn't good for the baby."

"We'll work as quickly as we can, sir. In the meantime, please try to keep everyone calm." Upton turned to me. "Jess, can I speak with you privately?"

I led him and Kyle to the small dining area near the kitchen, away from the crowd in the living room. Officer Roberts stayed behind, already pulling out his notepad to begin taking statements.

"Let me see the security footage," Upton said.

I pulled out my phone and opened the security app. "I can pull up the footage from today."

"Good. Let's see what we've got."

I navigated to the front camera feed and scrolled back to around noon, when guests had started arriving. The three of us crowded around my phone screen, watching people come and go. Monte and Mallory arriving together. Noah and April. Granny Ines and Auntie Rita. Max. Elias. Everyone waving at the camera or chatting as they walked up the steps.

"There," Kyle said, pointing at the timestamp. "12:47. That's when Honey arrived."

We watched Honey's white van pull up to the curb. Honey got out, retrieved the cake from the passenger seat, and carried it carefully toward the house. The van remained parked at the curb.

"Keep going," Upton said.

I fast-forwarded through the next hour. More guests arriving. People going in and out to the patio. The twins running past the camera at one point, laughing.

Then, at 1:32, a figure appeared at the edge of the frame.

"Stop," Upton said sharply. "Go back."

I rewound and played it again. Someone approached from the left side of the screen, staying close to the neighboring townhouse. They were wearing dark clothes and a baseball cap pulled low. The angle made it impossible to see their face clearly.

The figure moved quickly to Honey's van, crouched down near the tires, and pulled something from their pocket. A knife, I realized with a sick feeling. They slashed the first tire, then moved around the vehicle, staying low.

"Can you zoom in?" Upton asked.

I tried, but the resolution wasn't good enough to make out any identifying features. The person was average height, possibly male but I couldn't be certain. Their movements were efficient, practiced. Someone who knew what they were doing.

After slashing all four tires, the figure pulled out what looked like a spray paint can and quickly wrote the message on the windshield. SHOULD HAVE SOLD. Then they disappeared back the way they'd come, staying close to the buildings where the camera angle couldn't follow.

"Smart," Kyle muttered. "They knew where the cameras were and how to avoid them."

"Which means they've been watching," Upton said. "Studying the area, planning this." He looked at me. "Remind me, how long have those cameras been up?"

"Since last spring. After everything that happened with the restaurant fire."

"And they're visible from the street?"

"Yes. We wanted them to be a deterrent."

"Then our suspect knew they were there and planned accordingly." Upton pulled out his phone. "I'm going to send this footage to the tech team, see if they can enhance it. But in the meantime, we need to canvass the neighbors. Someone might have seen this person coming or going."

We returned to the living room where Officer Roberts was still taking statements. He was talking to Monte and Mallory, who both looked worried but determined to help.

"I was inside the whole time," Monte was saying. "Didn't hear or see anything unusual until Honey screamed."

"Same here," Mallory added. "Though I did notice a car driving by slowly earlier, maybe around one? Dark colored sedan. I didn't think much of it at the time."

"Can you describe it more specifically?" Roberts asked, writing quickly.

"Not really. It was just, you know, a regular sedan. Maybe black or dark blue? I only noticed because it went by twice."

Roberts made a note to check traffic cameras in the area. Upton nodded approvingly.

"Officer Rafferty, let's start with the immediate neighbors," Upton said. "Jess, which units are most likely to have seen something?"

"Barb and Sandy in 1408," I said immediately. "They're two doors down and they notice everything. Plus, they have a front porch where they sit a lot."

"Perfect. Let's start there. Roberts, you continue with the guests here. Get contact information from everyone before they leave."

I watched through the window as Kyle and Upton walked down to 1408. I could see Barb opening the door, her face showing concern as Kyle explained the situation. The two women stepped out onto their porch, both talking and gesturing animatedly.

After several minutes, Kyle and Upton moved to the next townhouse, then the one after that. They worked their way down one side of Willow Lane, then crossed the street to canvas those neighbors as well.

Inside, the atmosphere had shifted from celebratory to tense. Riley's parents had taken her into the kitchen to get her some water and help her calm down. The twins sat with Granny Ines, who was quietly telling them a story in Spanish to distract them. Sawyer paced near the window, his jaw tight with barely contained anger.

"I can't believe someone did this," he said to no one in particular. "During a baby shower. With all these people here. The kids."

"Whoever it is, they're sending a message," Noah said quietly. "They don't care who sees. They want Honey to know they're serious."

Honey sat on the couch, staring at nothing. Shayla had brought her tea, but it sat untouched on the coffee table. April sat beside her, not saying anything, just being present.

"Did you get everything on the security footage?" Max asked me.

"Yeah. Someone in dark clothes and a baseball cap. They knew exactly where the cameras were."

"That's premeditated," Elias said. "This wasn't some random act of vandalism."

"No," I agreed. "It wasn't."

Kyle and Upton returned twenty minutes later, both looking frustrated.

"What did the neighbors say?" I asked.

"Barb and Sandy saw someone walking down the street around 1:30, but they were on the phone and didn't pay much attention. Said it looked like someone in workout clothes, maybe going for a jog. By the time they looked up again, the person was gone."

"What about the other houses?"

"We're checking traffic cameras now. As for the neighbors, only two other units on this street have security systems, and neither caught anything useful. Their cameras face different directions."

Honey finally spoke, her voice hollow. "This is about Clark's deadline, isn't it? Tomorrow. He said his offer was good until tomorrow."

"We're definitely looking at Mr. Marlowe as a suspect," Upton said carefully. "But we need evidence before we can make any arrests. Right now, all we have is a vandalized vehicle and a threatening message."

"And the bee attack," Kyle reminded him. "And multiple threats sent to Jess and Honey."

"All of which point to someone who wants Honey to sell her property. But wanting something and committing crimes to get it are two different things in the eyes of the law. We need proof."

Officer Roberts finished with the last guest and joined them. "I've got statements from everyone. A few people noticed small details, nothing that gives us a clear suspect. But the consensus is that whoever did this was watching the house, waiting for the right moment."

"Which means they could still be watching," Vee said quietly.

The thought sent a chill through the room. I looked around at all the people I loved, gathered in what should have been a safe space for celebration. My gaze landed on the twins, huddled close to Granny

Ines, their faces still pale from the scare. They'd been through so much already in their short lives. First losing their parents, then adjusting to life with me, the nightmares after past cases. And now this. They deserved safety, stability, normalcy. Not this constant threat hanging over us. Instead, they were trapped inside, giving statements about a crime that happened right outside while they ate cake and opened presents.

"I want a patrol car on this street 24/7," Upton said to Kyle. "Rotating shifts. And Jess, I strongly recommend you and your household consider staying somewhere else until we catch whoever's doing this."

"We're not leaving our home," I said firmly.

"Then at least be extra vigilant. Keep your security system armed, don't go anywhere alone, and call immediately if you see anything suspicious."

"What about me?" Honey asked. "Should I accept Clark's offer? Just to make this stop?"

"That's your decision," Upton said. "But I wouldn't recommend making major life choices based on threats and vandalism. That just shows whoever's doing this that their tactics work."

"But what if they escalate again? What if next time someone gets hurt?"

"We're going to increase patrols. Have cars driving by your farm and bakery every hour instead of every few hours. And we're going to catch whoever's doing this."

"Thank you," Honey said quietly.

By three o'clock, Upton and Roberts had finished their initial investigation. They'd collected paint samples from the message on the windshield, taken detailed photos of the tire slashing, and documented everything from multiple angles. A tow truck had been called to take Honey's van to the police impound lot as evidence.

After the police left, guests began trickling out. Everyone hugged Riley and Sawyer, apologizing that their special day had been ruined.

Roy and Linda offered to stay and help clean up, but Sawyer insisted they go home and rest.

"We've got this, Mom," he said, hugging her. "Thanks for being here."

"Well, at least let me take some of this food home," Linda said, already reaching for containers. "You girls made so much, and Roy loves quiche."

"Of course," I said, packing up portions of the quiche and some sandwiches for them.

Riley's parents were hovering near their daughter, Diana still fussing. Victor gently tried to guide her toward the door, but Diana wasn't ready to leave yet.

"You should take some food too," Vee said to them. "We have plenty."

"Oh, we couldn't," Diana protested, but Victor was already accepting the containers Vee handed him.

"Riley needs to eat well for the baby," Granny Ines said, wrapping up a generous slice of the Russian honey cake. "And this one is good for energy." She tucked it into a bag along with some fruit salad. Then she cut another slice for herself. "Rita and I will have a piece later tonight. We can't let Honey's beautiful cake go to waste."

Auntie Rita nodded in agreement. "It's too good not to enjoy, even after such a day."

Finally, Diana allowed Victor to guide her to the car, their arms full of containers.

Once everyone was gone, we tackled the cleanup. Vee, Shayla, and I worked on putting leftover food into containers and stacking them in the fridge. The quiche Shayla and I had made that morning went into one container, the remaining sandwiches into another. There was still plenty of fruit salad, cheese and crackers, and of course, the beautiful Russian honey cake that Honey had brought.

"Riley and Sawyer should take most of this home," Vee said, wrapping up generous portions of everything. "They barely got to enjoy their own party."

"Good idea," I said, finding a large bag to pack it all into.

Riley and Sawyer gathered all the gifts to take home. The beautiful carved sign from Roy was carefully wrapped and placed in their car along with bags of baby clothes, blankets, and other necessities for their daughter.

Before they could head out, Sawyer touched my arm. "Can I talk to you for a second?"

"Of course."

He glanced around the crowded living room, then gestured toward the kitchen. "Let's grab some privacy."

We moved to the far end of the kitchen, away from everyone else, near the back door. I could see the worry lines etched around his eyes, the tension in his shoulders. This was the guy who'd been my best friend since we were twelve years old. We'd grown up together, lived together, built our adult lives side by side. He knew me better than almost anyone.

"I'm worried about you," he said, his voice low and serious. "Are you, Vee, and the girls safe? I mean really safe?"

"Sawyer—"

"Because if you're not, if there's even a chance something could happen, I need you to tell me. Do you need me to stay?"

I looked at my best friend, this man who was about to become a father, who had his own family to protect now. The urge to say yes, to keep him close like we'd always been, was strong. But that wasn't fair to him or Riley.

"You need to be with Riley," I said firmly. "We'll be fine. There will be an officer outside at all times until this is over. Kyle's arranging it right now."

He looked past me toward the living room where Riley was talking with Shayla and Vee, one hand on her belly. His expression was torn between duty to his chosen family and responsibility to the family he was creating.

"If you're sure," he said, but I could hear the doubt.

I reached out and took his hand, squeezing it. "I'm sure." I smiled at him, trying to project more confidence than I felt. "Besides, you've got more important things to worry about right now. Like figuring out how to change diapers and survive on no sleep."

That got a small smile from him. "I still can't believe I'm going to be a dad."

"You're going to be a wonderful father, Sawyer. That little girl is so lucky to have you."

His eyes got a little shiny, and he pulled me into a tight hug. "We've been through a lot together, Jess. Since we were kids. I don't know what I'd do if something happened to you."

"Nothing's going to happen to me," I said, hugging him back just as tight. "I'm too stubborn, remember?"

He laughed, a wet sound, and pulled back. "Yeah, you are." He wiped his eyes quickly. "Okay. But you call me if anything changes. Anything. I don't care what time it is."

"I will. I promise."

We walked back to the living room together. Riley looked up as we approached, reading something in Sawyer's expression.

"Everything okay?" she asked.

"Yeah," Sawyer said, wrapping an arm around her. "Everything's okay."

"Thank you so much for today," Riley said, hugging me tightly. "Despite everything, it was beautiful."

"I'm just sorry it ended the way it did."

"Not your fault. We'll remember the good parts." Riley smiled, one hand on her belly. "And this little girl will hear all about it someday."

I handed them the bag of leftovers. "Take these. You barely got to eat at your own party."

"Oh, you didn't have to do that," Riley protested, but she took the bag gratefully.

After they left with their car loaded with gifts and food, the house felt quieter. The twins had already retreated to their room, exhausted from the day's drama. A few stray balloons clung to the ceiling, and the kitchen counter still held some wrapped cake.

Kyle had stayed, quietly helping finish the cleanup. His presence was both comforting and a reminder of how serious the situation had become.

That evening, after the twins were in bed and Shayla had retreated to her room, Vee, Kyle, and I sat in the kitchen with coffee.

"This is escalating faster than I expected," Kyle said. "The vandalism in broad daylight, with dozens of witnesses nearby. That takes either desperation or confidence."

"Or both," Vee added.

"We need to figure out who's behind this before someone gets hurt," I said. "The threats, the bees, now this. What's next?"

"That's what worries me," Kyle admitted. "Each incident has been more brazen than the last. Whoever's doing this isn't afraid of getting caught. Or they're so desperate they don't care anymore."

"What about the security footage? Can your tech team really enhance it enough to identify who it was?"

"Maybe. Depends on how good the original resolution is and what angles we can work with." Kyle paused, thinking. "Though you know who might be able to help if our guys can't?"

"Who? Cullen?" I asked.

"Yeah, he's got connections with some of the best tech specialists around. If anyone can enhance that footage, he can find someone who will."

"That's a good idea," I said. "I'll reach out to him tomorrow if your team comes up empty."

"It's worth a shot."

My phone buzzed with a text. Unknown number again.

Unknown: You should have minded your own business. Now everyone you love is a target.

I showed it to Kyle, who immediately took a photo of the screen.

"That's it," he said, standing up. "I'm staying here tonight. On the couch. And I'm calling for that 24/7 patrol car starting right now."

"Kyle, you don't have to do that."

"Yes, I do. Because whoever sent that text just made this personal." His jaw was set in that stubborn way I had come to recognize. "And I'm not letting anything happen to you or anyone else in this house."

As Kyle made calls to arrange the patrol car and Vee went upstairs to check on Shayla and the twins, I stood alone in the kitchen. The remains of the baby shower surrounded me. A few balloons deflating slowly in the corners. Half a Russian honey cake, each layer a testament to Honey's skill and love, now just a reminder of how quickly celebration could turn to fear.

Tomorrow was Clark Marlowe's deadline. And I had a terrible feeling that whoever was behind all of this wasn't done yet.

Chapter Eighteen

The scream pierced through the quiet house at 2:47 AM.

I bolted upright in bed, my heart pounding. For a split second, I couldn't place the sound, then it came again. High-pitched, terrified, unmistakably Ivy.

I threw off my covers and ran for the stairs, nearly colliding with Vee who'd burst out of her room at the same time. We thundered down the steps together, my bare feet hitting the cold floor as I rushed toward the twins' room.

Another scream joined the first. Dove, crying and wailing.

Shayla was already there, sitting on the edge of Ivy's bed, trying to gather the thrashing child into her arms. Ivy was sobbing, her eyes wide and unseeing, still caught in whatever nightmare had gripped her.

"No, no, no!" Ivy screamed. "Don't take us! Please don't take us!"

"Ivy, sweetie, it's okay. You're safe. You're home." Shayla's voice was gentle but firm, trying to break through the panic.

Dove sat up in her bed across the room, tears streaming down her face, her whole body shaking. "What's happening? What's wrong with Ivy?"

I went straight to Dove, pulling her into a tight hug. "It's okay, baby. Ivy just had a bad dream. She's going to be okay."

But Dove was spiraling too, her breathing coming in short gasps. "Is someone coming? Are they going to hurt us?"

"No, no one's coming. You're safe. I promise you're safe."

Kyle appeared in the doorway, still in his jeans and t-shirt from earlier, his hair mussed from sleeping on the couch. He took in the scene quickly, then moved to help Shayla with Ivy.

"Hey there, Ivy. Can you look at me?" His voice was calm, steady. "That's it. Look right here at me. Can you tell me five things you can see?"

Ivy's wild eyes found his face. She was still crying, but the screaming had stopped.

"Five things you can see," Kyle repeated gently. "Take your time."

"You," Ivy choked out between sobs.

"Good. That's one. What else?"

"Shayla."

"Two. Keep going."

"My... my nightlight."

"Three. You're doing great."

"The... the poster. With the butterflies."

"Four. One more."

Ivy looked around the room, her breathing starting to slow. "Dove. I can see Dove."

"Perfect. Five things. Now, can you tell me four things you can touch?"

It was a grounding technique I had seen Dr. Martinez use with the twins during their therapy sessions. The fact that Kyle knew it made my heart squeeze.

Slowly, methodically, Kyle walked Ivy through the exercise. Four things she could touch. Three things she could hear. Two things she could smell. One thing she could taste.

By the time they finished, Ivy's breathing had mostly returned to normal, though tears still streaked her face. Dove had calmed too, watching her sister with worried eyes while I held her close.

"What was the dream about?" Shayla asked softly, smoothing Ivy's hair back from her damp forehead.

"Bad people were coming," Ivy whispered. "Like... like before. When Grandma Lynn had those people with the guns." Her voice broke. "They were coming to take us away from you."

Shayla's eyes filled with tears. "Oh, baby. No one's taking you anywhere. You're staying right here with me. Forever."

Even though the twins had never witnessed any of that, it still held an impact. Their young minds had filled in the blanks, creating terrifying images of what might have happened. Sometimes I thought that was worse. At least if they'd seen it, we'd know exactly what they were processing. But this way, their imaginations could conjure up scenarios far more frightening than reality.

"But what about the person who hurt Miss Honey's car? What if they come here?"

"They won't," Kyle said firmly. "There's a police officer outside right now, watching the house. And I'm here too. Nobody's getting past us."

"Promise?" Dove asked from my arms.

"I promise."

Vee had disappeared during the grounding exercise, and now she returned with two cups of warm milk. "Here, girls. This will help you feel better."

The twins accepted the cups, sipping slowly. The room felt heavy with the weight of everything they'd been through. Their mother and stepfather shot execution style in their own home. Their grandmother Lynn and father Ezra orchestrating the murders from prison. Being placed with Lynn temporarily, who'd seemed sweet until everything unraveled. And then, just weeks ago, being held hostage by Zane while he threatened to kill me. And now, today's violence had opened all those old wounds.

"I think," Shayla said quietly, "I'm going to sleep in here tonight. Would that be okay?"

Both twins nodded eagerly.

"Can Jess and Vee stay too?" Ivy asked in a small voice.

"We're right upstairs," I said. "But we can leave your door open, and if you need us, you just call out. We'll be here in two seconds flat."

"I'll be on the couch," Kyle added. "Right outside your door. Anyone wants to get to you, they have to go through me first."

That seemed to reassure them. Shayla settled into Ivy's bed while Ivy climbed in with Dove. The two girls curled up together, holding hands.

"Can you leave the hall light on?" Dove asked.

"Of course," Vee said, adjusting the nightlight and leaving the door cracked open.

We filed out quietly, leaving Shayla to whisper softly to the girls. In the hallway, I leaned against the wall and let out a shaky breath.

"That was intense," Vee whispered.

"They've been doing so well," I said, wiping at my own eyes. "I thought we were past the worst of it."

"Trauma doesn't work like that," Kyle said gently. "Dr. Martinez warned you there would be setbacks, especially when new scary things happen."

"I know. I just hate that they have to go through this. They're eight years old. They should be worried about spelling tests and butterfly projects, not whether someone's going to hurt them."

"They're lucky to have you three," Kyle said. "The way you all responded, the way Shayla knew exactly what they needed. That's not nothing."

Vee yawned. "I'm going back to bed. Jess, you okay?"

"Yeah, I'm fine. Go sleep."

After Vee disappeared upstairs, Kyle turned to me. "You're not fine. You're shaking."

"I'm just... wound up. Adrenaline."

"Come on. Let's make some tea."

In the kitchen, Kyle put the kettle on while I sat at the island, my hands still trembling. The house was quiet except for the soft murmur of Shayla's voice drifting from the twins' room.

"You were really good with them," I said. "The grounding technique. Where'd you learn that?"

"Training. We use it with people in crisis all the time." He poured hot water over tea bags. "Kids, adults, doesn't matter. When someone's panicking, you need to bring them back to the present moment."

"Well, it worked. Thank you for being here."

"I'm glad I was." He handed me a mug of chamomile tea. "Are you going to be able to sleep?"

"Probably not. My brain won't shut off."

"Mine either."

We sat in comfortable silence, sipping tea. The clock on the microwave read 3:24 AM. In a few hours, the sun would rise and it would officially be Clark Marlowe's deadline day.

"What do you think is going to happen tomorrow?" I asked.

"Honestly? I don't know. But I'm hoping we get something from the security footage. Or one of the neighbors remembers something useful." Kyle ran a hand through his hair. "We're missing something. I can feel it."

"What do you mean?"

"Three suspects, all with clear motives. But none of them quite fit. Clark's too obvious. The Douglas couple seems too desperate and scattered. And May..." He trailed off.

"What about May?"

"I don't know. Something's not adding up with her. The financial situation, the partnership agreement, the way she's been acting. But she doesn't seem like someone who could pull off something this calculated."

"Maybe she had help?"

"Maybe." Kyle checked his phone. "I'm going to make some calls in the morning. See if forensics found anything on Honey's van. Check if there are any new leads."

"And in the meantime?"

"In the meantime, we stay alert. Keep everyone safe. And hope whoever's behind this makes a mistake."

I finished my tea and stood to rinse the mug. Through the kitchen window, I could see the patrol car parked across the street, but I didn't see Officer Blair in the driver's seat. He must be doing a walking patrol of the block.

"I should try to sleep," I said, though I didn't move toward the stairs.

"Jess, it's okay to be scared."

"I'm not scared for me. I'm scared for them." I gestured toward the twins' room. "For Shayla, for Honey, for everyone caught up in this mess. Someone out there is willing to destroy lives to get what they want, and we don't even know who they are."

"We will. I promise you, we will figure this out."

Kyle headed back to the couch, and I finally climbed the stairs to my room. But I knew I wouldn't sleep. My mind was too active, cycling through everything that had happened. The baby shower. The vandalism. The threatening texts. Ivy's screams.

I changed into sweatpants and a hoodie, then paced my room. Back and forth, back and forth, trying to burn off the anxious energy thrumming through my body.

At 4:15 AM, I gave up on even trying to sleep. I went to my window and looked out at the street. The patrol car was still there, but the driver's seat was empty. Officer Blair must still be on his walking patrol.

The neighborhood looked still and peaceful.

Except.

I froze, my hand on the curtain.

There. At the edge of the glow from the streetlight. A shadow that didn't belong.

I watched, barely breathing, as the figure moved along the parked cars on our side of the street. They were dressed in dark clothes, moving carefully, quietly. Checking car doors? Looking in windows?

The figure paused at Vee's car, tried the handle. It didn't open. They moved to my car next.

My heart hammered in my chest. I grabbed my phone and typed quickly to Kyle.

Me: Someone outside. Checking cars. Can you see from the living room?

The response came back immediately.

Kyle: On it. Stay inside.

Seconds later, the porch light flicked on. The figure outside seemed to sense something because they suddenly went still, then started moving faster.

The front door opened. Kyle stepped onto the porch.

"Police! Stop right there!"

The figure bolted, running down the street away from the patrol car. Officer Blair appeared from between two townhouses, his radio crackling. He sprinted to his cruiser, and a moment later the headlights flashed on and it lurched forward. Kyle was already running down the steps.

I flew down the stairs, ignoring Kyle's instruction to stay inside. By the time I reached the front door, both Kyle and Officer Blair were chasing the figure down Willow Lane.

Lights were coming on in neighboring houses. Someone shouted. A dog started barking.

The figure cut between two townhouses and disappeared into the shadows.

I stood on the porch, my breath coming in short gasps, watching Kyle and Officer Blair search the area with flashlights. After several minutes, they returned, both breathing hard.

"Lost them," Kyle said, frustration clear in his voice. "They knew the area too well. Had an escape route planned."

"Did you get a look at them?" I asked.

"Not a good one. Average height, dark clothes, baseball cap. Same description as our vandal from earlier."

"They were checking our cars," I said. "Trying the doors."

"They must have been watching," Officer Blair said, breathing hard. "Waiting for me to step away on patrol. I was only gone five minutes."

"That's all they needed," Kyle said grimly. "They've been studying our patterns."

Kyle pulled out his phone and called it in. Within minutes, two more patrol cars arrived. Officers began searching the area more thoroughly, checking between houses, looking for any sign of the prowler.

By now, Vee and Shayla had come out, both looking worried. The twins appeared in the doorway behind them, holding hands.

"What's happening?" Shayla asked.

"Someone was outside," I said. "Trying to get into our cars. Kyle and Officer Blair chased them off."

"Oh my God." Shayla pulled the twins back inside. "Girls, back to bed. Now."

"But what if they come back?" Ivy's voice was high and scared.

"They won't," Kyle said firmly, coming up the steps. "We've got four patrol cars out here now. Nobody's getting near this house."

Upton's car pulled up, followed by Officer Roberts. The detective looked tired and angry as he climbed out.

"Someone want to tell me what the hell is going on?" he asked, walking up to the porch.

Kyle filled him in while I stood there, my arms wrapped around myself. The sky was starting to lighten in the east. Dawn would come soon, bringing with it Clark Marlowe's deadline.

"This is escalating too fast," Upton said after Kyle finished. "First the vandalism at the party, now someone prowling around the house at night. Jess, I'm going to ask you again. Please consider staying somewhere else until we catch this person."

"We have eight-year-old twins who just woke up screaming from nightmares," I said. "Moving them to another location right now would make things worse, not better."

"Then we increase security. Round-the-clock protection, not just patrol cars driving by."

"We don't have the manpower for that," Kyle said quietly.

"Then we make it happen. I'm not waiting for someone to get hurt." Upton pulled out his phone. "I'm calling the chief. We need more resources on this."

As Upton walked away to make his call, I looked at the street. Neighbors were out on their porches now, talking in quiet voices. Barb and Sandy from 1408 stood on their front steps in bathrobes, looking concerned.

The sun was coming up on what was supposed to be just another Monday. But I had a sinking feeling it was going to be anything but ordinary.

Someone had come to our house in the middle of the night. Had tried to get into our cars. Had been bold enough to wait and watch for the exact moment when Officer Blair stepped away on patrol.

Whoever was behind all of this was getting desperate.

And desperate people were dangerous.

Chapter Nineteen

The officers were still searching the area between townhouses when Upton's radio crackled to life.

"All units, we have a structure fire at 4892 County Road 15. Honey J's Farm and Flowers. Fire department en route. Reports of animals in danger."

Upton's head snapped up. "That's Honey Jacobson's property."

I felt my stomach drop. "No. No, not the farm too."

Kyle was already moving toward his patrol car. "Upton, I'm responding."

"We all are. Roberts, Blair, with me." Upton turned to me. "You need to stay here."

"I'm coming with you," I said firmly. "Honey's going to need support. A friendly face."

"Jess, this is an active emergency scene."

"I know. I promise I'll stay back. I won't interfere. But please, she's been through so much already. Let me be there for her."

Upton studied my face for a long moment, then nodded curtly. "You stay in the car until we secure the scene. Understood?"

"Understood."

"I'll stay here," Officer Blair said. "Keep an eye on the house and the girls."

I ran inside to tell Vee and Shayla what was happening. They were both in the living room, drawn downstairs by the commotion outside.

"Honey's barn is on fire," I said quickly. "I'm going with the officers. Blair's staying here to watch the house."

"Go," Vee said immediately. "We've got the twins. They're still asleep."

"Be careful," Shayla added, worry creasing her face.

I grabbed my jacket and ran back outside, climbing into the back of Upton's sedan. Kyle and Roberts were already pulling out in their patrol cars, lights flashing but sirens off to avoid waking the entire neighborhood.

The drive to the farm felt endless, though it was only about fifteen minutes. Dawn was breaking, painting the sky in shades of pink and orange that would have been beautiful under any other circumstances. As we turned onto County Road 15, I could see the smoke rising in the distance.

"Oh God," I breathed.

We pulled up to find the barn fully engulfed in flames. Fire trucks were just arriving, firefighters jumping out and beginning to unroll hoses. Then I saw Honey.

She was running toward the barn, screaming.

"My goats! They're still inside! I have to get them out!"

Kyle intercepted her, grabbing her around the waist and physically holding her back. "Honey, no! You can't go in there!"

"But they'll die! Please, they'll die!" Honey was fighting him, trying to break free, her voice raw with panic and desperation.

I jumped out of the car, forgetting my promise to stay back. I ran to Honey, taking her hand. "Honey, listen to me. The officers will get them out. You can't help them if you're hurt."

"There are still twelve inside," Honey sobbed. "I got a few out, but I couldn't get the rest. I raised them from babies. I can't lose them too. Not after the bees. Please!"

Roberts and two firefighters were already approaching the barn with protective gear. Through the smoke and flames, I could hear the terrified bleating of the goats trapped inside.

"How many are in there?" Roberts shouted to Honey.

"Twelve! Please hurry!"

The firefighters had gotten water on the flames near the barn door, creating a path. Roberts and another officer ran inside, and moments later emerged with two panicked goats. Then back in for more.

Honey counted each one as they came out, her whole body shaking. "One, two, three, four..."

Kyle had released her but stayed close, ready to grab her again if she tried to run. I kept hold of her hand, squeezing tight.

"Five, six, seven, eight..."

The flames were growing worse. Part of the roof collapsed with a shower of sparks. Honey screamed.

"There are still four in there! Please!"

Roberts disappeared back into the smoke. The wait felt like forever. Then he emerged, coughing, with two more goats. A firefighter followed with another.

"Eleven," Honey counted, her voice breaking. "There's one more. One more. Please, please, please."

Kyle started forward, but the fire chief grabbed his arm. "Too dangerous. The whole structure's about to come down."

"No!" Honey wailed. "No, please, I can't leave her! She's just a baby!"

But then Roberts came out one more time, carrying a small white goat in his arms. He was coughing hard, his face covered in soot, but he had the goat.

"Twelve," Honey gasped. "Twelve. You got them all."

She collapsed to her knees, sobbing with relief. I knelt beside her, wrapping my arms around her as she cried.

The goats milled around in confused panic, but they were all alive. All twelve, bleating and scared but breathing. The firefighters began herding them away from the burning structure, toward the front yard where they'd be safe.

With a tremendous crash, the barn's roof collapsed entirely. Flames shot up into the early morning sky, and the firefighters increased their water flow, working to contain the blaze and keep it from spreading to the farmhouse or the surrounding fields.

Honey watched it burn, tears streaming down her face. Then something shifted in her expression. The devastation hardened into something else. Something fierce.

"Now I'm ready to fight," she said, her voice low and dangerous. "Whoever did this, whatever they want, I don't care anymore. I'm not backing down. I'm not selling. I'm going to find out who's doing this, and I'm going to make them pay."

I had never heard Honey sound like that. The sweet, gentle woman who talked about her bees like they were her children had been pushed too far.

"Honey," Upton said, approaching carefully. "I need to ask you some questions. When did you discover the fire?"

"Maybe twenty minutes ago? I couldn't sleep, so I came out to check on the goats. I do that sometimes when I'm anxious. I saw the flames and called 911." She wiped her eyes, smearing soot across her face. "The chickens are okay. They're in a separate coop on the other side of the property. But the barn... everything was in there. Tools, feed, supplies, my tractor. Everything."

"Did you smell any accelerant?" Kyle asked. "Could you smell gasoline or anything like that?"

"I don't know. I just saw fire and ran to get the goats out. I managed to get the door open and lead out a few before it got too bad, but then the smoke..." She started coughing, and one of the paramedics who'd arrived with the fire trucks came over to check on her.

"Ma'am, you need to let me look at you. Smoke inhalation is serious."

While the paramedic examined Honey, Upton, Kyle, and Roberts huddled together. I stayed close enough to hear.

"This is arson," Upton said quietly. "Has to be. The vandalism at the baby shower, the prowler at Jess's house, and now this? All in less than twenty-four hours?"

"Whoever's doing this is escalating fast," Kyle agreed. "They're getting desperate."

"Or confident," Roberts added, still coughing slightly. "They set this fire knowing the fire department would respond, knowing we'd all be here. They don't care about getting caught."

"Or they think they're too smart to get caught," Upton said grimly.

A car came speeding up the gravel drive. May's sedan skidded to a stop, and she jumped out, her eyes wide.

"Oh my God, Honey! Are you okay?" May ran toward us, her face a mask of concern. "I saw the smoke from the road. What happened?"

"Someone burned down my barn," Honey said flatly, accepting an oxygen mask from the paramedic.

"Burned? You mean like arson?" May's voice pitched high. "Who would do that?"

"That's what we're trying to figure out," Upton said, watching May carefully.

I watched too. Something about May's reaction felt off. She'd arrived awfully quickly. And while her face showed the right expressions of shock and concern, her body language seemed wrong.

Her eyes kept darting to the burning barn, then to Honey, then to her phone, which she kept checking compulsively.

"At least you're safe," May said, kneeling beside Honey. "And the goats made it out. That's what matters."

"The barn's a complete loss," Honey said. "Everything in it. Do you know how much it costs to replace a barn? All those tools? The tractor alone was worth fifteen thousand dollars."

"The insurance will cover it," May said quickly. Too quickly. "And honestly, Honey, maybe this is a sign. Maybe it's time to accept Clark's offer and just... move on. Start fresh somewhere else."

Honey's head snapped toward May, her eyes narrowing. "A sign? My bees are dead, my barn is burned to the ground, and you think it's a sign I should sell?"

"I just mean, with everything that's happening, maybe it's not safe to stay here. Maybe whoever's doing this won't stop until..." May trailed off, seeming to realize she'd said too much.

"Until what?" Honey asked, her voice cold. "Until I give up everything I've worked for?"

"I'm just trying to look out for you," May said, but she was backing away, uncomfortable under Honey's glare.

"Ms. Lowen," Upton said, "how did you know about the fire?"

"I told you, I saw the smoke."

"From where?"

"From... from the road. I was driving past."

"At six in the morning?"

May's face flushed. "I couldn't sleep. I was worried about Honey after everything yesterday, so I went for a drive. I just happened to be nearby when I saw the smoke."

"That's quite a coincidence," Kyle said, his tone neutral but his eyes sharp.

"I live ten minutes away," May said defensively. "It's not that strange."

But I noticed May's hands were shaking. And she kept glancing at her phone, as if expecting a call or message.

The fire chief approached, pulling off his helmet. "Detective Upton? We've got the fire under control, but you're going to want to see this."

We followed him around to the back of what remained of the barn. In the early morning light, I could see scorch patterns on the ground leading away from the structure.

"Multiple points of origin," the fire chief said, pointing. "Here, here, and here. Someone used an accelerant, probably gasoline, and set fires in three different spots. This wasn't an accident. This was intentional."

"How long would it take for the fire to spread with that much accelerant?" Upton asked.

"Fast. Maybe ten, fifteen minutes from ignition to full involvement."

Upton pulled out his phone and checked the time. "Honey called 911 at 5:47 AM. So, the fire was set sometime around 5:30 or 5:35."

"Still dark," Kyle noted. "Easy to approach without being seen."

"But risky," Roberts added. "Anyone could have driven by and spotted them."

"Unless they knew no one would be watching," Upton said, looking pointedly at May.

May's face went white. "What are you saying?"

"I'm saying it's interesting that you happened to be nearby when this fire started. That you're pushing Honey to sell right after she says she's going to fight back. That you seem more concerned about insurance money and Clark Marlowe's offer than about your partner almost dying trying to save her animals."

"That's not fair," May protested. "I care about Honey. I'm just being realistic about our financial situation."

"Our financial situation," Honey repeated bitterly. "You keep saying that. Like you're the one losing everything."

"I invested my life savings into this partnership," May said, her voice rising. "If the farm fails, I lose everything too."

"But if we sell to Clark, you'd make a profit," I said quietly. "Isn't that right?"

All eyes turned to me. Upton gave me a warning look, but I continued.

"Your partnership agreement lets you force a sale if the business becomes financially unviable. And with the bees gone and now the barn destroyed, the farm's value has tanked. But the land is still worth what Clark's offering. Maybe more."

May's face had gone from white to red. "How do you know about our partnership agreement?"

"Because it's public record," Kyle said. "And because we've been investigating everyone connected to this case."

"I didn't do anything," May said, but her voice wavered. "Yes, I want to sell. Yes, I need the money. But I didn't kill the bees, and I certainly didn't burn down the barn. Why would I? I need this farm to be worth something if we sell."

"The land is worth something," Upton said. "The structures and livestock? Those are liabilities to a buyer like Clark Marlowe. He wants the acreage, not the operation."

May opened her mouth, closed it, then opened it again. "I want a lawyer."

"That's your right," Upton said. "Officer Roberts, please take Ms. Lowen to the station. We'll continue questioning there once her attorney arrives."

"Am I under arrest?" May's voice was shrill.

"Not at this time. But we have questions, and you've requested counsel, so we'll do this properly at the station." Upton's tone was firm but not unkind. "You're free to follow Officer Roberts in your own vehicle, or he can transport you. Your choice."

"I'll drive myself," May said quickly.

"Roberts will follow you to ensure you arrive safely," Upton said, which we all knew meant to make sure she didn't run.

Roberts nodded and walked May toward her car. As they left, I could hear May saying, "I didn't do it, I didn't do it, I swear I didn't do it."

But she was crying. And that, more than anything, made me wonder what exactly May hadn't done.

Honey watched her partner leave, something broken showing in her eyes. "She's been my friend for three years. We built this together. How could she?"

"We don't know that she did," Upton said gently. "But we're going to find out."

As the sun fully rose over Honey J's Farm and Flowers, illuminating the smoking ruins of the barn and the traumatized goats huddled in the front yard, I realized that this case was far from over.

May was hiding something. But was she a perpetrator or just another victim of whoever was systematically destroying Honey's life?

And more importantly, if May wasn't behind the attacks, then who was?

Because whoever it was, they weren't done yet.

Chapter Twenty

After the last of the fire trucks left, I helped Honey clean up some of the debris that had blown onto the porch from the barn fire. It was mindless work, but it gave us something to do while we waited for news from the police station.

Honey had gone inside to make sandwiches for lunch, and I was sweeping ash off the porch steps when I noticed a crumpled receipt caught between the railing posts. It must have blown from one of the vehicles during all the chaos this morning. I pulled it free, intending to add it to the trash pile, when a line item caught my eye.

Heavy-Duty Protective Suit - $347.99

My pulse quickened. I smoothed out the receipt, reading the details. It was from an agricultural supply store in Pinehurst, dated six weeks ago. The payment method was listed as cash.

Six weeks ago. Right around the time someone had purchased a protective suit for handling dangerous insects, according to Kyle's investigation. Paid in cash to avoid a paper trail.

But whose receipt was this?

I looked at the bottom of the receipt where a name was printed: M. Lowen - Rewards Member #83749

May.

May had bought a protective suit six weeks before the bees were killed. May, who had entomology training. May, who would know how to handle Asian Giant Hornets safely. May, who stood to gain over a hundred thousand dollars if Honey sold to Clark.

My hands were shaking as I pulled out my phone and called Cullen.

"Hey, Chef, what's up?"

"Cullen, I need you to trace a purchase for me. Like, right now. It's urgent." I read off the store name, date, and transaction details from the receipt.

"Okay, give me a minute." I could hear him typing rapidly. "What am I looking for?"

"Proof that May Lowen made this purchase. The receipt shows rewards member number 83749. I need you to verify that it's registered to her and get security footage if you can access it."

"Got it. Hold on." More typing. "Okay, the store has digital records. Rewards member 83749 is registered to May Elizabeth Lowen. Purchase was made at 2:47 PM on that date, paid in cash. Security system is basic but... yeah, I can pull the footage. Give me two minutes."

I paced the porch, my mind racing. This was it. This was the evidence we needed. May had planned this weeks in advance, bought the protective equipment, acquired the hornets somehow, and systematically destroyed Honey's livelihood to force a sale.

"Got it," Cullen said. "Sending you the screenshot now. Check your phone."

I pulled up the image. It showed a clear view of May at a checkout counter, a large box labeled "Industrial Protective Suit" visible on the counter in front of her.

"Cullen, this is perfect. Can you send this to Detective Upton right away?"

"Already done. Sent it to both Upton and Rafferty. Anything else?"

"No, that's... that's everything. Thank you."

I hung up just as my phone buzzed with a text from Kyle.

Kyle: All suspects have been cleared. No solid evidence to keep them. Stay alert.

My stomach dropped. Cleared? How were they all cleared? He must not have seen Cullen's email yet.

Another text came through before I could respond.

Kyle: On our way back to you now.

I started typing: "May bought the protective suit. Cullen just sent proof."

But before I could hit send, I heard the sound of tires on gravel. A car was coming up the drive.

May's sedan.

My finger hit send on the partial message, then I quickly typed: "May is here"

I hit send just as May's car came into view and parked near the house.

"Honey!" I called toward the open door. "Come out here."

Honey emerged, carrying a plate of sandwiches. "What's wrong? Oh." She saw May getting out of her car. "What's she doing back here?"

"I don't know. Just stay calm." I slipped my phone into my pocket and moved to stand beside Honey on the porch.

May walked toward us slowly. Something about her posture was different. Her shoulders were back, her jaw set. She looked resolved.

"May," Honey said cautiously. "I didn't expect to see you again today."

"I bet you didn't." May's voice was flat, cold. She stopped at the bottom of the porch steps, looking up at us. "They let me go. Not enough evidence, they said. Funny how that works."

"That's good," Honey said, though she didn't sound like she meant it. "I'm glad they realized you weren't involved."

"Oh, but I am involved." May's hand went to her jacket pocket. When it emerged, she was holding a gun.

Honey gasped and dropped the plate of sandwiches. It shattered on the porch, but none of us looked at it.

"May, what are you doing?" I asked, trying to keep my voice steady.

"What I should have done from the start." May's hand was steady on the gun, pointing it at both of us. "If you had just taken Clark's offer, Honey. It was a good offer. A great offer. A way out of this partnership that's been drowning both of us for months."

"May, please put the gun down," Honey said, her voice shaking. "We can talk about this."

"Talk? We've done nothing but talk! I've tried to reason with you, tried to make you see sense. But you wouldn't listen. You just kept holding on to this stupid farm, this stupid dream, while I watched my life savings disappear."

"So, you killed my bees," Honey whispered. "You burned my barn."

"I did what I had to do." May's voice rose. "The hornets were supposed to be enough. You were supposed to realize you couldn't continue without them, that selling was the only option. But no, you decided to fight back. You decided to be difficult."

"So, you burned down my barn," Honey's voice was getting stronger, anger replacing fear. "You destroyed everything my grandmother and mother built. Three generations of my family's work."

"I had to escalate! You weren't getting the message!" May's composure was cracking, her voice becoming shrill. "Do you have any idea what I've invested in this place? Twenty-five thousand dollars of my life savings. Three years of my life. And for what? To watch you play farmer while the money bleeds away?"

"You could have just left the partnership," I said carefully. "You didn't have to destroy everything."

May's eyes snapped to me, and the gun shifted to point directly at my chest.

"And you." May's voice was venomous. "If you would have just minded your own business, none of this would have happened. She would have sold and that would be that, but no, the crime-fighting chef couldn't do that, could she? You had to investigate, had to ask questions, had to stick your nose into things that don't concern you."

"People trying to destroy someone's life concerns me," I said.

"I wasn't trying to destroy her life! I was trying to save mine!" May was fully yelling now, tears streaming down her face. "I'm thirty-four years old with no savings, no job prospects, and a mountain of debt because I believed in this stupid farm. I believed in you, Honey. I thought we were building something together. But you wouldn't listen to reason. You wouldn't see that we were failing."

"We weren't failing," Honey said. "The farm was doing fine until you killed my bees."

"Fine? We were barely breaking even! And that's before your precious honey production. The flower business isn't enough to sustain this place long-term, and you know it." May wiped her face with her free hand, the gun wavering slightly. "Clark's offer was our way out. We could have both walked away with money, with a future. But you were too proud, too stubborn, too attached to your family's legacy to see reality."

"Don't you dare bring my family into this."

"Why not? That's what this is really about, isn't it? This farm isn't about making money or building a business. It's about you holding onto the past, refusing to move forward." May's laugh was bitter. "Well, congratulations, Honey. You've got your farm. What's left of it, anyway."

"May, please," I said, trying to pull May's attention back to me. Every second I could keep May talking was another second closer to Kyle arriving. "Put the gun down. You don't want to hurt anyone."

"Don't I?" May's eyes were wild and desperate. "I've already lost everything. My savings, my reputation, my freedom once they analyze that receipt you found."

My blood ran cold. "How did you know about the receipt?"

"I saw as I drove up. You were on the porch with your phone. I knew what you'd found." May's jaw clenched. "That was careless of me, leaving it here. I thought I'd picked up all the evidence when I left last time. But it doesn't matter now."

"It does matter," Honey said. "May, you can still stop this. You haven't hurt anyone yet. You can put the gun down and we can figure this out."

"Figure it out how? I killed all those bees with illegal insects I smuggled into the state. I committed arson. I've been threatening people, vandalizing property. There's no coming back from this." May's voice broke. "I just wanted my money back. I just wanted a chance to start over."

"By destroying everything I built," Honey said.

"You weren't building anything! You were playing pretend farmer while the real world passed you by!" May was fully sobbing now, but the gun never wavered. "I had plans, Honey. I was going to go back to school, get my master's degree, maybe teach at a university. But I needed capital. I needed the money from selling this place. And you wouldn't give it to me."

"Because this is my home," Honey said quietly. "This is my life."

"Well, now it's just ashes and dead bees." May took a step up onto the porch, and both Honey and I instinctively moved back. "And you know what the funny thing is? Clark's offer expires at midnight tonight anyway. So even if I'd succeeded in forcing you to sell, even if everything had gone according to plan, we're almost out of time anyway."

"Then let us go," I said. "If the offer's expiring, if it's already over, there's no point in this."

"No point?" May laughed, the sound unhinged. "The point is that I'm going to prison for the rest of my life. The point is that I destroyed myself trying to save myself. The point is that it's all over anyway, so what does it matter what happens next?"

In the distance, I could hear sirens. May heard them too. Her head snapped toward the sound, then back to us, her eyes widening with panic and rage.

"They're coming," May said. "Of course they're coming. The crime-fighting chef couldn't just stay out of it."

"May, please," Honey said, stepping forward with her hands raised. "Don't make this worse. You can still walk away from this."

"Walk away to what? A prison cell? A life I destroyed?" May's finger moved to the trigger. "No. If I'm going down, I'm not going down alone."

The sirens were getting louder. I could see dust rising from the road, multiple vehicles approaching fast.

May saw it too. Her face contorted with fury and desperation, and she raised the gun higher, pointing it directly at Honey's chest.

"You should have sold," May said, her voice cold and final. "You should have just sold."

Three patrol cars came screaming up the gravel drive, lights flashing. Kyle's car was in the lead. They screeched to a stop, and officers poured out, weapons drawn.

"Police! Drop the weapon!" Kyle's voice rang out clear and commanding.

May spun toward them, the gun now pointing at the officers. I grabbed Honey and pulled her behind the porch railing, trying to put something, anything, between us and the line of fire.

"Stay back!" May screamed. "Stay back or I'll shoot!"

Kyle held up one hand, the other on his weapon. "May, there's nowhere to go. You're surrounded. Please put the gun down."

"So you can arrest me? So I can spend the rest of my life in prison?" May's voice cracked. "I'm already dead. My life is over."

"It doesn't have to be," Kyle said, taking a slow step forward. "But if you hurt someone, if you pull that trigger, there's no coming back from that. Right now, you're looking at property crimes. Don't add murder to the list."

"Property crimes that will send me away for years anyway." May was backing up, still on the porch, the gun sweeping between Kyle and where Honey and I crouched behind the railing. "What's the difference?"

"The difference is you haven't hurt anyone yet," Upton's voice called from behind the patrol cars. "You can still walk away from this with a chance at a future. But not if you pull that trigger."

May stood frozen, the gun shaking in her hand. Tears streamed down her face. She looked at Honey, at me, at the officers surrounding her with weapons drawn.

"I just wanted my life back," she whispered. "I just wanted a second chance."

"Then take it," Kyle said gently. "Put the gun down and take your chance. Don't throw it away by doing something you can't undo."

For a long moment, nobody moved. The only sound was May's ragged breathing and the distant bleating of the goats in their temporary pen.

Then May's arm started to lower, the gun pointing at the porch floor instead of at people.

"That's good, May," Kyle said, taking another step forward. "Nice and slow. Just set it down."

May's hand was shaking violently now. The gun wavered, rose slightly, then lowered again.

And then her finger moved on the trigger.

Chapter Twenty-One

"May, don't!" Kyle's voice cut through the air. "Please, don't do this."

May's hand trembled, the gun jerking up and down. Her finger stayed on the trigger, but she didn't pull it. Not yet.

"Everyone back!" she screamed, her voice cracking. "Everyone just back off!"

The officers held their positions, weapons trained on her. Upton had moved to the side, trying to get a clearer angle. Roberts was on the other side, doing the same. They were surrounding her, cutting off any escape routes.

"May, listen to me," Kyle said, his voice steady and calm despite the situation. "I know you're scared. I know you feel trapped. But there's still a way out of this that doesn't end with anyone getting hurt."

"There's no way out!" May's eyes were wild, her whole body shaking now. "Don't you understand? I'm going to prison. My life is over. Everything I worked for, everything I sacrificed, it's all gone!"

"That's not true," Upton called. "You cooperate with us, tell us everything, show remorse, and that goes a long way with prosecutors. You could be looking at a reduced sentence, maybe even probation for some of the charges."

"Probation?" May laughed, the sound manic and wrong. "For arson? For smuggling dangerous insects? For threatening people? You think I'm stupid?"

"We think you're desperate," Kyle said. "And desperate people make bad choices. But you're also smart, May. Smart enough to know that pulling that trigger makes everything worse."

"Worse for who? Me? How could it possibly be worse for me?" May's voice was getting higher, more frantic. "I've already lost everything! My savings, my reputation, my freedom. What else is there to lose?"

"Your life," Honey said quietly from behind the railing. "May, please. You still have your life. Don't throw that away too."

May spun toward Honey's voice, the gun swinging wildly. I instinctively pulled Honey down further behind the railing.

"My life?" May's laugh was bitter. "What life, Honey? The one where I go to prison for destroying my business partner's livelihood? Where I spend the next ten, fifteen, twenty years in a cell, thinking about how I ruined everything?"

"Better than dead," Honey said.

"Is it?" May's voice broke. "Is it really?"

"Yes!" Honey stood up despite me trying to pull her back down. "May, I'm angry at you. I'm furious. You killed my bees, you burned my barn, you've terrorized me for weeks. But I don't want you dead. I don't want anyone dead."

"You should." May was crying openly now, ugly sobs that shook her whole body. "You should hate me. You should want me to suffer like I made you suffer."

"I do hate what you did," Honey said. "But you're still the woman who helped me plant three hundred flower bulbs in one day. Who stayed up all night with me when that baby goat was sick. Who laughed until she cried when we accidentally used salt instead of sugar in the cookie dough."

May's face crumpled. "Don't. Don't do that."

"You're still the May I worked beside for three years. The May who had dreams and plans and a future." Honey took a step forward, and this time I didn't try to stop her. "You made terrible choices, May. You did horrible things. But you're not a murderer. Not yet. Don't become one now."

"I can't go to prison," May whispered. "I can't. I'll die in there."

"You won't," Kyle said. "My friend served three years for embezzlement. She got out, went to therapy, and turned her life around. She's a counselor now, helping other people who've made mistakes. There's always a chance to rebuild, May. Always."

But May was shaking her head, backing further onto the porch. The gun was still in her hand, still pointing in our general direction, her finger still on the trigger.

"You don't understand," she said, her voice getting more frantic. "You can't understand. I had everything planned. Go back to school, get my doctorate, teach at Texas A&M like I always wanted. But I needed money. I needed capital. And this farm was supposed to give me that."

"I know," Honey said. "I know you had plans. I know you sacrificed a lot."

"Everything. I sacrificed everything!" May's voice was rising again, becoming manic. "My apartment, my car, my emergency fund. I put every penny I had into this partnership because you said it would work. You promised it would be worth it!"

"I didn't promise anything," Honey said quietly. "I told you farming was risky. That it would take time to build."

"Time I didn't have!" May was screaming now, completely hysterical. "I'm thirty-four years old with student loans and no savings and no prospects. I needed this to work, Honey. I needed it!"

May's head swiveled toward me, her eyes unfocused and wild.

"Can you tell me five things you can see?" I asked, my voice calm and steady.

"What?" May's face scrunched in confusion.

"Five things you can see. Right now. Just look around and tell me five things."

"Why?" May's voice was suspicious, but some of the manic energy had dimmed slightly.

"Because I want you to breathe. I want you to focus. Can you do that? Five things you can see."

May blinked, looking around almost against her will. "I see... police cars."

"That's one. Good. What else?"

"The... the goats. In the yard."

"Two. Keep going."

May's breathing was starting to slow, just slightly. "Honey. I see Honey."

"Three. You're doing great. Two more."

"The barn. What's left of it." May's voice cracked.

"That's four. One more. What else do you see?"

May looked around, and her eyes landed on the farmhouse. "The porch swing. The one Honey's grandmother made."

"Perfect. Five things. Now, can you tell me four things you can touch?"

"What is this?" May asked, but she sounded more confused than angry now.

"It's grounding. It helps when you're overwhelmed. Four things you can touch."

May looked at the gun in her hand, then slowly reached out with her other hand to touch the porch railing. "The railing."

"Good. That's one."

"My jacket." May touched the fabric.

"Two. Keep going."

"The gun." May's voice was barely a whisper.

"Three. One more."

May's free hand went to her face, touching her wet cheeks. "Tears."

"Four things. You're doing so well, May. Now, can you tell me three things you can hear?"

May closed her eyes, listening. When she spoke, her voice was calmer. "The goats. They're bleating."

"That's one."

"The wind. In the trees."

"Two. One more."

"My heartbeat. It's so loud in my ears."

"That's three things. Almost done. Can you tell me two things you can smell?"

May inhaled shakily. "Smoke. From the barn."

"One more."

"Honey's lavender. She always smells like lavender."

Honey let out a small sob at that.

"Perfect. Last one, May. Can you tell me one thing you can taste?"

May's face crumpled. "Salt. From crying."

"One thing you can taste. You did it, May. You made it through." I took a small step forward. "Now, can you look at the gun in your hand?"

May looked down at it, and something shifted in her expression. The manic desperation had faded, replaced by exhaustion and grief.

"I don't want to die," May whispered. "I'm so scared, but I don't want to die."

"Then don't," I said gently. "Put the gun down, May. Just set it on the porch and step away from it."

"But they'll arrest me."

"Yes. They will. And you'll face consequences for what you did. But you'll be alive. You'll have a chance to make this right, to maybe rebuild someday. But only if you're alive."

May stood frozen, the gun hanging loosely in her hand. Then, slowly, she bent down and placed it on the porch floor. She straightened up, raised her hands, and started sobbing.

"I'm sorry," she choked out. "I'm so sorry. For everything."

Kyle moved quickly, securing the gun while Roberts came up behind May and gently guided her hands behind her back to cuff her.

"May Lowen, you're under arrest for first-degree arson, agricultural bioterrorism, making terroristic threats, illegal importation of dangerous animals, multiple counts of vandalism and trespassing, stalking, and assault with a deadly weapon. You have the right to remain silent..."

As Roberts read May her rights and led her to his patrol car, Honey collapsed onto the porch steps. I sat down beside her, and we watched as May was placed in the back of the police car.

"It's over," Honey said, her voice hollow. "It's actually over."

"Yeah. It's over."

Kyle came over to us, his face exhausted but relieved. "That was incredible, Jess. The grounding technique. I saw what you were doing. From this morning, with Ivy."

"It worked for her," I said with a small smile. "I thought maybe it would work for May too."

Kyle looked moved. "You remembered. In the middle of all that chaos, with a gun pointed at you, you remembered and stayed calm enough to walk her through it." He shook his head in amazement. "That took incredible courage."

"She didn't want to hurt anyone," I said. "She was just desperate and scared and felt like she had no options. The grounding helped her see clearly again."

Upton approached, his expression a mix of relief and exasperation. "Well, that was about ten years off my life. Good work though, Jess. You probably saved lives today."

"I just did what Kyle taught me," I said.

"Still." Upton looked at Honey. "Ms. Jacobson, I'm going to need a detailed statement from you. But that can wait until tomorrow if you need time to process everything."

"Tomorrow," Honey said, not taking her eyes off the patrol car where May sat in the backseat, her face buried in her cuffed hands. "I can't do this today."

"Understood." Upton turned to Kyle. "Rafferty, take Jess home. I'll stay here and coordinate with the fire marshal. We need to process the barn site as evidence now that we have our suspect."

"What about Clark's offer?" Honey asked suddenly. "It expires at midnight tonight."

"Let it expire," Upton said. "With May's arrest, Clark's going to have a lot of questions to answer about his timing and his knowledge of the situation. I don't think he was directly involved, but I'd stay far away from any business dealings with him if I were you."

Honey nodded. "I never wanted to sell anyway. I just wanted to be left alone to run my farm."

"You will be now," Upton said. "I promise you that."

Kyle nodded and touched my shoulder. "Come on. Let's get you back to the twins and Shayla. They're probably worried sick."

On the drive back to Willow Lane, I stared out the window, my mind replaying the confrontation. May's desperate face, the gun wavering in her shaking hand, the moment when the grounding technique had broken through her panic.

"You okay?" Kyle asked quietly.

"I don't know. I feel... I don't know." I rubbed my face. "She did terrible things. She could have killed someone. But I also understand how she got there. The desperation, the feeling that you have no options."

"That doesn't excuse what she did."

"I know. But it makes it more tragic somehow." I looked at Kyle. "She destroyed her own life trying to save it."

"A lot of criminals do," Kyle said. "They make one bad choice, then another trying to cover up the first one, then another. Before they know it, they're in so deep they can't see a way out."

"Do you think she'll get a fair sentence?"

"I think she'll get what she deserves. Which, given the severity of the charges, is probably fifteen to twenty years. Maybe less with good behavior and cooperation." Kyle paused. "Still a long time, but she'll have a chance at life after."

"Twenty years," I breathed. "She'll be in her fifties when she gets out."

"If she gets out earlier with good behavior. And she showed remorse, surrendered peacefully. That counts for something." Kyle glanced at me. "But she committed serious crimes, Jess. Agricultural bioterrorism, arson, assault with a deadly weapon. The law has to mean something."

When we pulled up to the townhouse, Vee, Shayla, and the twins came running out. The twins launched themselves at me, hugging me tight.

"We were so scared!" Ivy said.

"Officer Blair told us there was a dangerous situation," Dove added.

"I'm okay," I said, hugging them both. "Everything's okay now."

Vee pulled me into a tight embrace once the twins let go. "Don't ever do that again. When Blair told us you were in a standoff with an armed suspect, I thought I was going to lose my mind."

"Sorry. I didn't exactly plan it."

"Did you catch the bad guy?" Dove asked.

"We did," Kyle said, giving both girls a gentle pat on the head. "And Jess helped. She used that grounding technique I taught you, Ivy. Remember? Five things you can see?"

Ivy's eyes went wide. "You used that on the bad guy?"

"I did. And it worked."

"Cool!" Both twins said in unison.

Shayla was crying, hugging me tight. "I thought we were going to lose you. After everything we've been through, I thought..."

"I'm here. I'm safe. We're all safe." I held her, then pulled back to look at all of them. "And May is in custody. It's over."

Inside, we gathered in the living room. Kyle stayed for a while, making sure everyone was settled and answering the twins' questions about what had happened, carefully editing out the most frightening parts.

"So, the lady who hurt Miss Honey's bees was just really sad and scared?" Ivy asked.

"Yes," Kyle said. "Sometimes people do bad things because they're desperate and can't see any other way. That doesn't make it okay, but it helps us understand why it happened."

"And she's going to jail now?"

"Yes. For a long time."

"Good," Dove said firmly. "She shouldn't hurt people's bees."

Later, after the twins were in bed and Shayla had retreated to her room, I sat with Vee and Kyle in the kitchen over coffee.

"What happens now?" Vee asked.

"May will be arraigned, probably tomorrow," Kyle said. "She'll be charged formally, and then it's up to the courts. Given the severity of the crimes, she's looking at fifteen to twenty years, possibly more depending on how the prosecutor handles the bioterrorism charges."

"And Honey?" I asked.

"She'll have to rebuild. The insurance should cover the barn, and she's already contacted a bee supplier about getting new colonies. She wants them established before the main bloom season hits." Kyle smiled slightly. "She's tougher than she looks."

"She'll need help," I said.

"And she'll have it. The whole town will rally around her once word gets out about what happened." Kyle looked at me. "Including you, I imagine."

"Of course. That's what friends do."

Kyle's phone buzzed. He checked it and sighed. "Upton needs me back at the station. We're going to be processing evidence and doing paperwork for hours." He stood up, then paused and looked at me. "What you did today, the way you talked May down, that was incredible. You probably saved lives."

"I just remembered what you taught me."

"You did more than that. You stayed calm under pressure, you read the situation, and you found the right approach when tactical solutions weren't working." He squeezed my shoulder. "That's all you."

After Kyle left, Vee and I sat in comfortable silence for a while.

"I can't believe it's over," Vee finally said. "Honey's bees, the barn, all those threats. And it was May the whole time."

"Yeah. Working alone, just trying to force a sale so she could get her money back."

"It's sad, really. She destroyed everything, including herself, for money she'll never get now."

"That's the tragic part. If she'd just been honest with Honey, if she'd just asked to dissolve the partnership legally, they might have worked something out. But she got desperate and made everything worse."

"Do you think Clark really didn't know what was happening?"

"I think he suspected something. The timing of his offers, the way he kept pushing. But I don't think he was directly involved. He's just an opportunistic vulture, not a criminal." I sipped my coffee. "Though Upton will probably keep investigating him just to be sure."

"And the Douglas couple?"

"Same. Desperate but not criminal. Well, not criminal in this case anyway." I smiled slightly. "Their bakery will probably still fail, but at least they're not going to prison."

"Unlike May."

"Unlike May," I agreed softly.

We sat in silence again. I couldn't stop thinking about May's face when she'd broken down, when the grounding had brought her back to reality and she'd realized what she was about to do.

"You know what the saddest part is?" I said. "May had real skills, real talent. She could have done so many things with her life. But she let desperation drive her choices, and now all those possibilities are gone."

"For at least fifteen to twenty years, anyway."

"Yeah. Maybe she'll use that time to figure out who she wants to be when she gets out. Get therapy, work through her issues, come out better on the other side."

"Maybe," Vee said, though she didn't sound convinced. "Or maybe she'll just be bitter and broken."

"I hope not. I hope she finds some kind of peace, even in prison." I stood up and stretched. "But right now, I just want to hug my family and be grateful we all made it through this in one piece."

"Amen to that," Vee said, standing too. "Though I could use about twelve hours of sleep first."

"Same. Let's hope the twins sleep through the night after all this excitement."

As if on cue, we heard a small voice from the hallway.

"Jess?" Ivy stood in her pajamas, clutching her stuffed butterfly. "Can I sleep with you tonight? I had a bad dream."

My heart melted. "Of course, sweetie. Come on."

Moments later, Dove appeared too, not wanting to be left out. We all ended up in my room, the twins curled up on either side of me, talking quietly about butterflies and school and anything except guns and standoffs and desperate people making terrible choices.

This was what mattered, I thought as the twins finally drifted off to sleep. Not solving crimes or catching criminals. This. Family. Safety. Love.

Everything else was just details.

Tomorrow we'd deal with statements and evidence and the aftermath of May's arrest. Tomorrow Honey would start the long process of rebuilding. Tomorrow life would continue with all its complications and challenges.

But tonight, we were all safe. All together. All okay.

And that was enough.

Chapter Twenty-Two

One Week Later

The kitchen at The Crock Pot smelled like heaven. Garlic, herbs, and slow-roasted chicken filled the air as I checked the oven temperature and stirred the soup of the day. Tomato basil, my old standby. Simple, comforting, predictable.

I smiled as I ladled a taste. Perfect.

"Chef, table six needs their order," Marco called from the expo station.

"On it." I plated the chicken and dumplings with practiced efficiency, adding a perfectly placed sprig of parsley on top. "Order up!"

It felt good to be back in my routine. After a week of chaos, disrupted schedules, police statements, and emotional exhaustion, the rhythm of service was exactly what I needed. Easy. Predictable. Therapeutic.

"You seem more relaxed today," Eli observed from his station beside me. "Actually relaxed, not just faking it."

"I am relaxed," I admitted, grateful for my reliable cook who always had my back. "I missed this. Just cooking, just being here without worrying about bees or barns or people with guns."

"Can't blame you for that." Eli seasoned a chicken breast with smooth, confident movements. "Though I have to say, what you did was pretty incredible. Talking that woman down like that."

"Just glad nobody got hurt."

"Still. That took guts." Eli slid the chicken onto the grill. "The crime-fighting chef strikes again."

I groaned. "Please don't call me that."

"Too late. It's already a thing. Monte's even making t-shirts."

"He's what?"

"Kidding. Probably." Eli laughed at my expression. "But seriously, you did good. That Honey lady gets to keep her farm, and that May person gets help instead of hurting someone. That's a win."

I supposed it was. May was in custody, awaiting trial. Her lawyer was negotiating a plea deal that would likely result in fifteen to twenty years in prison with mandatory therapy. Not ideal, but better than life in prison or someone getting killed.

The lunch rush continued, and I lost myself in the familiar dance of cooking. Searing, stirring, plating, tasting. This was my happy place. This was where I belonged.

By two o'clock, the rush had died down, and I was finishing up my prep when my phone buzzed. A text from Honey.

Honey: You should see what's happening at the farm! Come by when you can!

I showed the text to Noah. "Mind if I leave a bit early? Honey wants me to come by. I can still pick up the twins on time."

"Go ahead. We're covered." Noah smiled. "Tell her we're all thinking of her."

"Will do."

Twenty minutes later, I pulled up to Honey J's Farm and Flowers and stopped short at what I saw.

The farm was packed with people. Trucks, cars, and vans lined the gravel drive. In the space where the barn had burned down, a new structure was rising. Not finished yet, but the frame was up, and people were everywhere, hammering, sawing, painting.

And at the center of it all, directing traffic with a clipboard and a measuring tape, was Clark Marlowe.

I got out of my car slowly, trying to process what I was seeing.

Honey spotted me and came jogging over, her face flushed with happiness and exhaustion.

"Can you believe this?" Honey gestured at the controlled chaos. "They all just showed up this morning. Clark called and said he was bringing a crew to help rebuild. I thought he meant like three or four people. But look!"

I counted at least twenty people working on various parts of the barn. Some were locals I recognized, others I didn't.

"Clark's doing this?" I asked, still stunned.

"He said it was his way of apologizing. That he didn't mean for things to escalate the way they did, that his pushiness and his offers gave May the idea that he'd support what she was doing." Honey's eyes were bright with tears. "He's paying for all the materials, and he brought his whole construction crew. Said he wants to make it right."

Clark noticed us and walked over, wiping sweat from his forehead.

"Ms. Vasquez," he said with a nod. "Didn't expect to see you here."

"I could say the same," I replied carefully.

Clark had the grace to look embarrassed. "Yeah, well. I've been thinking a lot this past week. About how my behavior, my constant pushing, might have given May ideas. Made her think I'd be okay with what she was doing."

"You didn't know what she was doing," Honey said quickly.

"No, but I wasn't exactly subtle about wanting this land. And I sure as hell wasn't kind about it." Clark looked at the barn frame. "My daddy always said, 'If you break it, you fix it.' Well, I didn't break your barn, but I helped break your peace of mind. So, I'm fixing what I can."

"The barn will be done by the end of the week," Honey said, squeezing my arm. "And it's going to be even better than the old one. Bigger, better ventilation for the animals, proper storage for equipment."

"And fireproof," Clark added gruffly. "Got special treated lumber, installed fire suppression system. Nothing's burning this one down."

I felt my throat tighten. "That's really generous of you, Clark."

"It's what neighbors do." Clark shifted uncomfortably, clearly not used to being praised. "Now if you'll excuse me, I need to make sure those idiots aren't installing the support beam backwards." He stomped off, bellowing instructions.

"He's actually kind of sweet under all that gruffness," Honey said with a small smile.

"I never thought I'd hear you say that."

"Neither did I. But he's been here since six this morning, working harder than anyone. And when I tried to thank him, he just said, 'Shut up and let me fix my mistake.'" Honey laughed. "I'm starting to think he's not as bad as I thought."

We walked around the property, Honey pointing out the progress on the barn and the temporary shelters they'd set up for the goats. The chickens were still in their coop, happily oblivious to all the drama.

"What about the bees?" I asked.

"Ordered three new colonies yesterday. They'll arrive next week, just in time for the late spring bloom." Honey's expression turned determined. "I'm starting over. New bees, new barn, new attitude. May tried to destroy everything I built, but all she really did was make me realize how strong I am. How strong this community is."

A car pulled up, and Abby and Dale Douglas got out, both carrying boxes.

"Oh good, you're still here!" Abby called out. "We brought lunch for everyone!"

She and Dale set up a folding table and started unpacking sandwiches, cookies, and drinks. I noticed the boxes were from Dreamy Desserts.

"We're organizing a bake sale fundraiser next weekend," Abby explained as she arranged the food. "All proceeds go to Honey to help with rebuilding costs and replacing the bees. We've already got commitments from a dozen local businesses to donate items."

"That's incredibly generous," Honey said, looking touched.

"It's the least we can do," Dale said quietly. "We weren't exactly supportive when you were going through all this. We were so wrapped up in our own problems. We didn't think about how to be good neighbors."

"Plus," Abby added with a sheepish smile, "the positive publicity from organizing the fundraiser has been amazing for our bakery. We've had more customers this week than we've had in months. People want to support businesses that support the community."

"Win-win all around," I said.

"Exactly." Abby handed Honey a sandwich. "And we're really sorry we couldn't be better friends to you during all this."

"You're here now," Honey said simply. "That's what matters."

As people broke for lunch, gathering around the makeshift table to eat and talk, I felt a wave of warmth wash over me. This was what community meant. Not perfection, not always getting it right the first time, but showing up when it mattered. Helping fix mistakes. Supporting each other through the hard times.

My phone buzzed. A text from Vee.

Vee: **What's for dinner tonight?**

I smiled and typed back.

Me: **Tacos and enchiladas. I've got everything covered.**

Vee: **Perfect. See you at home!**

I pocketed my phone and turned to Honey. "I should get going. But this is amazing, Honey. Really amazing."

"Thank you for everything, Jess. For supporting me, for putting yourself in danger to help me, for just being a friend." Honey hugged me tight. "I couldn't have gotten through this without you."

"That's what friends do."

Before I left, I stopped at Honey's farm stand and picked up a loaf of honey wheat bread and some honey cookies for dessert. Honey insisted on not charging me, but I left money on the counter anyway when she wasn't looking.

As I drove toward Dashwood Elementary, I thought about the past week. The terror of having a gun pointed at me, the exhaustion of giving statements to police, the worry about the twins and their nightmares. But I also thought about the community coming together, the support they'd shown Honey, the way even people like Clark and the Douglases had stepped up to make things right.

May would face consequences for what she'd done. That was justice. But this outpouring of support and rebuilding? This was healing.

At 3:15, I pulled up to Dashwood Elementary just as the bell rang. The twins came running out, their backpacks bouncing.

"Jess! Jess!" Ivy called. "Guess what? I got a hundred on my math test!"

"That's amazing!" I hugged her as she climbed into the car. "I'm so proud of you."

"And I finished my butterfly project!" Dove added from the backseat. "Want to see when we get home?"

"Absolutely. I can't wait."

The drive home was filled with their usual chatter about school, friends, and the playground. They were calmer now, sleeping through the night without nightmares. Dr. Martinez said they were processing everything really well, and it showed in moments like this, just normal kid stuff, no fear or trauma shadowing their joy.

At home, I got them settled with snacks and homework at the kitchen table. I had about an hour before I needed to start dinner, and I spent it helping Ivy with math problems and admiring Dove's butterfly project.

Vee came home at her usual time, still in her postal uniform. "How was everyone's day?"

"Good! Jess went to see Miss Honey's new barn!" Ivy reported.

"The whole town is helping rebuild it," I explained. "Clark Marlowe is running the whole project."

"Really? That's unexpected."

"Right? But it's actually really nice to see." I started pulling out ingredients for dinner. "How was your day?"

"Busy. Friday always is." Vee grabbed an apple slice from the twins' snack plate. "But good. Normal."

Normal. That word kept coming up, and I realized how much I'd missed it.

Shayla got home from the bakery around five-thirty, and we all worked together to make dinner. Tacos and enchiladas, always a crowd-pleaser. By six o'clock, we were gathered around the table, talking and laughing about our days.

After dinner and cleanup, Kyle stopped by with ice cream to go with the honey cookies I had picked up. We ate dessert together, the twins showing him their homework and butterfly pictures.

"Things feel settled," I said to Kyle quietly while the twins played in the living room. "Like we can finally breathe again."

"That's good. You all deserve some peace." Kyle smiled. "And for what it's worth, you handled everything incredibly well. Not just the standoff but taking care of everyone through all of it."

"I had help," I said, glancing toward the living room where Vee was helping the twins build a pillow fort.

By eight o'clock, the twins were in their pajamas, teeth brushed and tucked into bed. I read them a story about butterflies, and both girls were asleep before I finished the last page.

Later, after Kyle had left and the twins were asleep, I sat on my bed with Lulu curled up beside me and Baxter stretched across my feet. I pulled out my phone and scrolled through the photos from earlier. The new barn rising at Honey's farm. Clark directing his crew. Abby and Dale setting up lunch. The community coming together.

After everything that had happened, after coming so close to losing so much, I felt the need to acknowledge what I still had. To count my blessings, as Granny would say. I'd never been one for gratitude journals or writing things down like this, but tonight it felt important. Necessary, even.

I opened my notes app and created a new entry.

Things I'm Grateful For:

- My restaurant and the therapy of cooking
- Friends who are family
- A community that shows up when it matters
- Second chances (even for people like Clark and the Douglases)
- Twins who are healing
- Quiet, normal evenings at home
- The fact that nobody died, despite everything

I read over the list, feeling the truth of each line settle into my chest. Then I closed the app and set my phone on my nightstand.

Tomorrow I'd go back to work, lose myself in the rhythm of service, create beautiful food for hungry people. The twins would go to school and come home with stories about their day. Shayla would work at the bakery. Vee would sort mail at the post office.

Normal, beautiful, ordinary life.

I turned off the light and settled into bed, Lulu adjusting her position to stay close. Through my open window, I could hear the sounds of Dashwood at night. Distant traffic, crickets, the occasional dog barking.

I was home. I was safe. Everyone I loved was safe.

And for now, that was more than enough.

THE END

Before you go: If you loved Honey and Homicide, be sure to visit my website to sign up for my newsletter (if you haven't already) and to stay up to date on new releases and other bookish things.

When signing up, you will receive **Chef Jessica's Alphabet Soup Recipe** as a free gift. I have "had" it; it is yummy. (Okay, so obviously, it is my recipe, but still, I recommend it!)

Continue to the next section for this book's recipe!

Also, check out my other books! You can find links on my website.

www.ejwheltonwrites.com

Recipe:

This is a Medovik a Russian Honey cake. I didn't want to change the recipe because of the tradition of this cake. It symbolizes warmth, family gatherings and festive celebrations, which is why I picked it for Sawyer and Riley's baby shower.

The cake was actually a lot easier to make than I had thought. It also wasn't overly sweet. It was a perfect flavor. I hope if you make it, you enjoy it too!

Ingredients:
For cake:
3 large eggs
1 cup granulated sugar
1/2 cup honey
1/2 cup unsalted butter
1 1/2 tsp baking soda
3 1/2 cups all-purpose flour

For cream filling:
2 cups sour cream
1 cup heavy cream
3/4 cup powdered sugar
1 tsp vanilla extract

Directions:
1. In a heatproof bowl over simmering water, whisk together eggs, sugar, honey, and butter until the mixture becomes warm and smooth. Remove from heat.
2. Stir baking soda into the warm mixture; it will foam slightly, indicating activation.
3. Gradually sift in the flour and mix until a soft dough forms. Divide the dough into 8 equal parts, wrap each in plastic wrap, and refrigerate for 30 minutes.

4. Preheat the oven to 350°F (175°C). Roll each dough piece on a floured surface into a thin round, about 8 inches in diameter.

5. Place each rolled dough onto a parchment-lined baking sheet and bake for 4-5 minutes until golden but still soft. Repeat for all layers.

6. For the cream filling, whip together sour cream, heavy cream, powdered sugar, and vanilla extract until smooth and creamy.

7. Once all cake layers have cooled, spread the cream evenly between each layer and stack the cake. Spread some cream over the top and sides.

8. Crumble any leftover scraps from trimming the cake layers and sprinkle on top as decoration.

9. Refrigerate the assembled cake for at least 6 hours, preferably overnight, to let flavors meld and cake soften.

Author note:

My oldest grandson has been really into bees and wasps, so he was talking to me one day about them. That is what gave me the idea to research what would kill honeybees and bam, Asian hornet.

I hated to "kill" the honeybees in this story. Rule number one is not to kill animals, but it really fit this story, and I think was a new twist for a murder investigation.

I hope you enjoy this story and the character development. Next, we'll have Iced Tea and Intrigue. I love iced tea, but I typically drink it unsweet which is almost a sin in Texas, but I just prefer it that way. Strong and bitter. But I do like flavored teas, so I'm looking forward to testing out new tea recipes.

Until next time, thank you so much and happy reading!

www.ejwheltonwrites.com